W9-CPA-103

LETHAL BAYOU

BEAUTY

Jana DeLeon

Lethal Bayou Beauty

Copyright © 2013 Jana DeLeon

Chapter One

I was right in the middle of a dream where I was Lara Croft, but not as girlie, when my cell phone rang. I sprang out of bed, grabbed my nine, and hit the floor in a firing stance, facing the bedroom door. Then I remembered I was hiding out in Sinful, Louisiana, and not on a CIA mission in the Middle East. I lay my nine back on the nightstand and reached for my cell phone.

Seven a.m.

I looked down at the display and saw it was Gertie, one of the seemingly quiet and unassuming seniors I'd met the day I arrived in the tiny bayou town. I'd thought when I came to Louisiana to hide from the arms dealer who had placed a price on my head that my biggest fear was being bored to death. Instead, the merry seniors and I had been chased by police, been stalked by a killer, killed the stalker, and solved a five-year-old murder.

And I'd only been in town five days.

"We have an emergency," Gertie said as soon as I answered. "Ida Belle and I are on our way over."

She disconnected the call before I could ask for any details, and I rushed into the bathroom to wash my face and throw on clothes. As I pulled on jeans and a T-shirt, I hoped nothing had happened to implicate Marie in her husband's murder. I'd thought she was safe after everything that had gone down the day before, but things in Sinful, Louisiana, had a way of shifting beneath you.

I ran downstairs at the same time Gertie's ancient Cadillac pulled up in my driveway. I unlocked and opened the door, then hurried into the kitchen to put on coffee. Conversations with Gertie and Ida Belle weren't good without something to drink. Given the strain in Gertie's voice, I thought whiskey might be a better option, but as it was only seven a.m. it was probably too early for good manners to take me straight to the bottle.

But I could always play that one by ear.

Ida Belle, the leader of the Sinful Ladies Society—a group referred to by Sinful citizens as The Geritol Mafia—was the first to enter the kitchen, and she did not look happy. But then, if I'd had that mass of rollers in my hair and had been prompted out of my house in my bathrobe, I probably wouldn't have looked happy either. Gertie trailed behind, her expression one of exasperation and worry. I figured the exasperation was due to listening to Ida Belle complain the entire two-block drive to my house.

Ida Belle glanced at the empty coffeepot and sighed, then slumped into a chair at the breakfast table.

"Sorry," I apologized for the coffee situation. "I was still sleeping when Gertie called."

Ida Belle waved a hand in dismissal. "Vampires were still sleeping when Gertie called. Damn woman is always awake at indecent hours."

"If you'd go to sleep at a normal time like other women your age," Gertie said, "you wouldn't have so much trouble getting up."

"I was busy waxing my car," Ida Belle grumbled.

Gertie rolled her eyes. "You and that car. I thought you said you were going to address your overly protective issues concerning that car."

I reached for coffee mugs. By the time they finished this age-old argument, the coffee should be ready. And I wasn't about to step into the middle of that fight. I had personal feelings about Ida Belle's car, and none of them were polite enough for seven a.m.

"For your information," Ida Belle said, "I was waxing it so that I can sell it."

I froze and stared. For the first time since I'd met her, Gertie ran out of words.

"Stop staring at me like I've lost my mind," Ida Belle said. "You two are the ones who accused me of having an unhealthy relationship with my car. This is all your fault, really."

I remained still and silent. Ida Belle was a crack shot and I couldn't be certain she wasn't packing, even in a bathrobe.

"Well," Gertie said, and wisely pushed her chair back an inch from Ida Belle's. "I guess I better get on with the business at hand then."

Change the subject. Good choice.

"The GWs met this morning at the crack of dawn," Gertie said.

I poured three cups of coffee and passed them to Gertie. "The who?"

"The GWs," Gertie said.

I slid into my chair and took a sip of coffee. "Do I even want to know what a GW is?"

"Probably not," Ida Belle said.

"The GWs are a local women's group," Gertie said.

"Doesn't Sinful already have enough trouble with the Sinful Ladies Society?" I asked. The SLS, led by Ida Belle, had been covertly running the town since the sixties.

"My society is not trouble," Ida Belle said. "We keep things running smoothly. But some of the women had issues with our admission requirements and decided to form their own club."

"Ah." I was starting to get the picture. Only old maids and women who'd been widowed for over five years could apply for membership in the SLS. They had a firm belief that the close proximity of men clouded logical thinking. I tended to agree.

"So what does GW stand for?" I asked.

Ida Belle rolled her eyes.

"God's Wives," Gertie said.

"I call them Got No Lives," Ida Belle interjected.

"I wish I could disagree," Gertie said, "as Ida Belle's sentiments are fairly rude, but unfortunately, all the GWs do is spend their time trying to get one over on the SLS. They don't really exist beyond that purpose."

"I see," I said. "So you're afraid the GWs met to plan their next strategic move in this Jurassic War?"

"Oh, I'm certain that's why they met. I wouldn't be here if I didn't have details."

I clenched a little. "Please don't tell me you've bugged their meeting place."

Since I'd discovered that Ida Belle and Gertie had been covert operatives during the Vietnam Conflict, it opened up all sorts of options that I normally wouldn't consider from your average senior citizen. They'd "made" me shortly after my arrival in Sinful, recognizing my military training, and had dedicated themselves to helping me maintain my cover. Unfortunately, they also expected me to take part in their spy-versus-spy shenanigans.

"Oh," Gertie perked up. "That's a great idea. We should really consider bugging the women's classroom at the Catholic church."

Ida Belle nodded. "Being friends with you is really paying off, Fortune."

I stared at them in dismay. "I didn't...I wasn't...never mind. Just don't tell me about it."

"So," Gertie continued, "I got the call this morning from Beatrice Paulson."

"Who's Beatrice Paulson?" I asked.

"Our spy," Ida Belle interjected. "Can you please keep up? I haven't had enough coffee to give a history lesson."

Gertie frowned at Ida Belle. "She can hardly know things she's never been told. No one is that good. Beatrice is our mole inside the GWs. She was widowed six years ago. So last year, when she was eligible for SLS membership, we turned her."

My head began to ache just a bit. "Are you sure that's safe? I mean, this Beatrice was a member of the other group for a long time, right? How do you know she's not feeding you false information?"

"She's clean," Gertie said. "After Selma passed and Celia took over leadership of the group, we knew Beatrice would jump at the chance."

"Celia Arceneaux?" I asked. "Of the Catholic-Baptist Banana Pudding Wars?"

Gertie nodded. "One and the same."

"I'm going to have to bring tennis shoes to church the entire time I'm here, aren't I?" I asked.

"Probably," Gertie said.

Ida Belle waved her empty coffee mug in the air and I jumped up to pour her another cup. "If you two are done reinventing the wheel, can we get on with this? I have to get these rollers out or I'll spend the entire week looking like a French poodle."

Gertie leaned toward us and lowered her voice. "Beatrice found out about the Summer Festival."

"Why the hell are you whispering?" Ida Belle asked. "Don't make me work this hard on two cups of coffee."

Gertie sighed. "Mayor Fontleroy agreed to their plan of having a children's beauty pageant."

Ida Belle looked as if she'd sucked on a lemon. "I'm not surprised given that idiot Fontleroy is Celia's ex-brother-in-law, but I don't have to like it. My idea for a shooting gallery would have been a lot more fun."

"Darn straight," I agreed.

"Apparently," Gertie said, "Idiot Fontleroy didn't think the shooting gallery was family-friendly."

"So do it yourself," I said, not understanding at all why this constituted an emergency. "I get that a beauty pageant makes you want to gag, but why not just do your own thing and ignore the rest?"

Gertie's eyes widened. "There can only be one main event at the Summer Festival."

I sighed. "Let me guess—having more than one main event is against the law?" Sinful had rewritten the book on absurd legalities.

Gertie nodded. "Of course. We manage to get our way some of the time because the mayor wants to appear impartial, even though he's not, but this one was a complete sweep for the competition."

"And why is that," Ida Belle asked, "when I know for a fact Fontleroy doesn't like Celia any more than we do, and the GWs got their sewing competition last year? It was our turn."

"That's the really, *really* bad part," Gertie said, "and why I called you straightaway. Pansy Arceneaux is coming back to town."

Ida Belle's eyes widened. "This is not good."

I frowned. The name sounded familiar and given that I'd been here less than a week and only knew a handful of people, that seemed odd. Then it clicked and I sucked in a breath.

"The beauty queen who went to Hollywood to get famous?" I asked. "She's Celia's daughter?"

"The one and only," Gertie said. "Pansy told Celia she wants to take a break from her hectic acting schedule, but I've kept an eye on the Internet Movie Database and know that's complete bull. More likely, she's broke and crawling home to Mama until she can get some more money out of her."

Instantly, my mind flashed back to the insipid Facebook page I'd found when trying to research the citizens of Sinful. "Okay," I said, "I can see why having her here would give one a serious butt rash, but why is that an emergency?"

"Because we have to work equally on the main event," Gertie said. "We're not allowed to duck out just because we don't like the featured activity."

Ida Belle nodded. "And with you being our new ally and *supposed* to be a former beauty queen yourself, you'll be expected to take the reins on this."

I sucked in a breath. Holy crap! This undercover situation was the gift that kept right on giving. Right now, it was giving me an ulcer. When CIA Director Morrow had informed me that I had a million-dollar price on my head, and a leak at the CIA had blown my cover, he'd thought my posing as his librarian/ex-beauty queen niece, Sandy-Sue, was the perfect solution.

Sandy-Sue had been scheduled for a summerlong visit to small-town Louisiana in order to settle up her great-aunt Marge's estate, but the real Sandy-Sue was jet-setting in Europe while I attempted—with limited success—to take her place in the strangest town on earth. Morrow had no idea just how many problems I'd run into in a town with less population than the high-rise I lived in back in DC.

Ida Belle studied me for a moment. "I suppose that glued-on hair of yours wasn't really due to a bleaching accident, was it?"

"No. I used to keep my hair about an inch long. It was easier that way given my line of work and the desert conditions."

Ida Belle shook her head. "Do you even own a brush? Know how to use a curling iron or apply mascara?"

I stared. "I'm not even certain what one of those is."

"This is not good," Ida Belle repeated.

"She'll just have to learn," Gertie said. "We have a couple of days and the Internet is full of information."

I shook my head. "You cannot make me a girlie girl in two days. Not to mention that I'd have to work with kids, something I have zero experience with. There are too many variables. It would be easier if I just killed her."

Ida Belle nodded. "She's right."

Gertie looked upward as if awaiting help from God. "You can't kill someone for being useless and annoying."

"Hmmpf," Ida Belle said. "Don't tell me the thought never crossed your mind when you had her in English class."

"Okay, maybe it did a time or two."

Ida Belle raised her eyebrows.

"Fine!" Gertie threw up her hands. "The girl was Satan's spawn and I've prayed every night since she left that she would be swallowed up in an earthquake if the thought of returning to Sinful ever crossed her mind. But none of that matters. What matters is that two days from now, Pansy will scrutinize Fortune worse than the IRS did Al Capone, and if we don't get her up to speed, it will blow her cover."

"Unfortunately, she's right," Ida Belle grumbled. "And I don't think the Internet is going to be enough ammunition to fix this situation."

"You have more ammunition than the Israeli

government," Gertie protested.

Ida Belle gave a long-suffering sigh. "*Knowledge* ammunition. You are I are not exactly fashion-forward. We wouldn't understand the half of what we saw or read any more than Fortune would. What we need is a professional."

Gertie frowned for a moment, then she brightened. "You're thinking about Genesis."

"Of course. Genesis is exactly what we need."

"I don't think even prayer is going to help this one," I said, "and I really see no reason to go all the way back to Genesis just to come up empty."

Gertie laughed. "Genesis Thibodeaux is a former Sinful resident who was only months away from SLS membership when she met Anton."

"Sacrilege," I said. "She ditched SLS membership for a man?"

"Not just any man," Gertie said. "Anton is intelligent, breathtaking, and immensely charming."

Ida Belle nodded. "So hot, he makes your eyes bleed. After the ladies met him, we couldn't exactly fault her."

"Too true," Gertie agreed. "Why if I were twenty years younger—"

Ida Belle waved a hand in dismissal. "You'd still be too damned old for him."

"Well, you don't have to be rude about it," Gertie pouted. "Anyway, Genesis is the perfect solution. She owns her own beauty shop and also does all the costumes, hair, and makeup for a theater company in New Orleans."

Ida Belle nodded. "If Genesis can't help you, no one can."

I took a big drink of coffee. I wasn't nearly as

confident as Gertie and Ida Belle, but I had to give it a try.

It seemed the only options were to start at the beginning with Genesis or end it all with Revelations.

Chapter Two

I cringed when we pulled up in front of the beauty shop. The storefront was painted fuchsia and purple and had giant yellow daisies scattered across the matching fuchsia awning.

"Are you sure about this?" I asked.

"Don't let the decor distract you," Gertie said.

"I'd have to go blind for this not to distract me."

"Got that right," Ida Belle grumbled. "Makes my butt itch, it's so loud."

Gertie waved a hand at Ida Belle. "The previous shop owner painted it this way, but it's sorta gained traction for being so loud and hideous. People will come into the shop simply because they want to see if anything odd is going on inside. Genesis gets a lot of new customers that way."

Gertie pulled open the door and I followed them inside. The interior of the shop was in sharp contrast to the outside. The floors were stone tile, the walls a light tan with paintings of New Orleans landmarks hanging on the wall. Each beauty chair had its own little area complete with a wall of mirrors and a wet bar. A row of recliners lined the front of the shop. A set of bookcases at the front of the store contained a good collection of books and magazines along with DVDs and several DVD players.

Okay, so the inside wasn't scary at all. In fact, I was seriously thinking about moving in for a day or two, when a door at the back of the shop swung open and a huge woman with more hair than any neck should be able to support came sauntering toward us.

Five-foot-three without the heels, two hundred forty pounds—twenty of which was the hair, high probability of type 2 diabetes.

She grinned at us and I studied her approach, amazed at how she kept all that weight centered on the six-inch, razor-thin heels she was wearing. I'd found that particular type of shoe handier for killing people than walking in, but apparently, Genesis didn't share the same prejudices.

She gave Ida Belle and Gertie both a hug, which mostly consisted of smashing them into her quite generous chest, and then turned her attention to me. I cringed inwardly, certain she was about to pummel me with her breasts, but instead, she narrowed her eyes and scanned me head to toe. I got the impression she was taking a mental inventory of weaknesses, like I did everyone, but with a completely different list of requirements.

Finally, she looked back at Ida Belle and Gertie. "Not bad."

Gertie beamed. "I told you."

Genesis looked back at me and nodded. "I can work with this."

"Her," I inserted. "I'm not a 'this.' And what's not bad? Does that mean it's good? It doesn't feel good."

Genesis narrowed her eyes at me. "How is it exactly that someone who ran the pageant circuit got so far off-field from beauty?"

"We always figured her mother was an awful liar." Ida Belle jumped in with the story she and Gertie had cooked up on the way to New Orleans. "Apparently, we were right."

I nodded. "She spent a lot of time talking about what she wanted me to be, not what I was."

Gertie added her two cents: "We just never realized how true that liar thing was until Sandy-Sue arrived and we got to know the real person, but we'd appreciate it if you keep all that on the down-low. We don't want to lose our edge against the GWs."

"Of course." Genesis blanched. "Sandy-Sue? She saddled you with Sandy-Sue?"

"Yes, but everyone calls me Fortune."

Genesis nodded. "I like Fortune. I can work with Fortune."

"Then you'd better hop to it," Ida Belle said, "because you've got a lot of work to do."

I couldn't even work up a decent glare. Ida Belle was right.

❧

Ten hours later, I slumped in the back of Gertie's ancient Cadillac, desperately wishing for a strong drink or death—maybe both, but in that order. I'd had more useless information thrown at me that afternoon than any one person should have to absorb in a lifetime. Lip gloss, eye pencils, eyelash glue, and an array of hair implements ran through my mind like a horror movie. Military weaponry was so much easier than this.

I closed my eyes, praying I could clear my mind enough to nap on the way home, when Ida Belle yelled over the seat.

"Wake up! We have work to do."

I opened one eye. "I've been working all day. I've conquered entire dictatorships with less effort."

"I'm not going to disagree with the sentiment," Ida Belle agreed, "as I've gone through an entire roll of Tums listening to that mess, but Gertie's been busy while you were being fluffed to death."

I felt a sliver of fear run through me. "Busy with what?"

Ida Belle held a handful of photos over the seat. "Making flash cards. We can work on your vocabulary on the way home."

She held up a photo of something long, thin, and metal that looked like a medieval torture weapon. "What's this?"

"Branding iron."

Ida Belle drew the card closer to her face, apparently reading something on the back. "Close. It's a clipless curling iron. How the hell do you hold your hair in that?"

"I have no earthly idea."

"Oh, I remember now," Ida Belle said. "You wear that Michael Jackson glove."

Gertie frowned. "I don't remember Michael Jackson being mentioned."

I closed my eyes again. It was going to be a very long ride home.

◦◦◦◦

"This is not good," Ida Belle grumbled as we approached my house.

"You're going to wear out that expression." I

didn't even bother to rise from my prone position on the backseat. "I don't care what it is. Just kill me and shove me in the bayou. No matter what, death will be easier."

"I hate to agree with her," Gertie said, "but in this case, she's probably right."

Since Gertie rarely agreed that death was the best alternative, I pushed up on one elbow and peered over the back seat as Gertie slowed to a crawl. "What is it?"

"Celia and Pansy just pulled into your driveway," Gertie said.

Ida Belle glared at Gertie. "Why is Pansy here already? I thought you said we had a couple of days."

Gertie looked as stressed as I felt. "We've got to move forward with bugging their meeting room. Our intel is getting sketchy."

I groaned. "Well, drive away or something. They can't see me back here, so it's not like they'll know I'm avoiding them."

"Yes, they will," Gertie said. "Francine knows we all went to Genesis' shop today. I picked her up some conditioner."

"Great," Ida Belle grumbled. "Ten minutes after we left town, everyone who ate at Francine's Café knew, then they went home and told everyone who didn't eat at Francine's Café."

I shook my head, still marveling at small-town happenings. "A trip to the hairdresser is big news? Really?"

"Word of the beauty pageant has probably made it around Sinful by now," Gertie explained. "Everyone will be wondering what we're going to do to counter Pansy's involvement. You're the natural choice, so yes, a trip to the hairdresser is big news."

"You people really need to get some hobbies."

"The murder investigation didn't help," Gertie added. "Especially since Ida Belle and I kinda pulled you into the middle of it. The spotlight was already on us. Now, it's just worse with the whole beauty pageant thing."

"Then let's get it over with," I said and pushed myself completely upright as Gertie pulled up to the curb in front of the house.

I recognized Celia immediately from the banana pudding race last Sunday, but wouldn't have pegged the woman standing beside her as her daughter by looks alone.

Five-foot-ten, thin but no muscle tone, the expected fake boobs, enough hair for five women.

Seriously, there must have been ten pounds of massive blond curls piled on top of her head. Between the hair and the enormous breasts, I was surprised she could stand without tilting forward. Maybe she had a little more muscle tone than I'd originally thought—at least in her neck and shoulders.

Celia stood right next to her, a short, dark-haired, flat-chested woman who didn't seem to share a single attractive feature with her daughter. Maybe Pansy was adopted. As we got out of the car and approached them, Pansy looked me up and down, then smirked. That expression exactly matched the one her mother had been wearing since we pulled in the drive. Definitely related.

"Gertie, Ida Belle," Celia nodded as we

approached. "I heard you were off in New Orleans for a day of beauty. I guess that didn't include the two of you."

"Beauty goes much deeper than skin," Ida Belle said, "but then, you wouldn't know that."

I shook my head. "Do you people actually listen in church or just go there so that you have the right to eat lunch at Francine's?"

"I listen in church," Gertie said, "and I still have my manners." She waved a hand at Pansy. "This is Pansy Arceneaux. Pansy, this is Sandy-Sue Morrow, but everyone calls her Fortune."

I took a step forward and stuck my hand out, anxious to get it over with. "Nice to meet you."

Pansy stared down at my hand as if it were a snake. I looked down, wondering what the problem was. All those horrible fake nails I'd pulled off when I'd arrived in Sinful were back in place, no thanks to Genesis, and were painted Sunshine Tangerine. I understood if *I* grimaced while looking at my hands, but didn't see what Pansy had a problem with.

"Ladies don't shake hands," she said finally.

"I'm sorry," I said as I drew my hand back. "No one told me you were a lady."

"Ha!" Ida Belle let out a single cry and Gertie kicked her in the shin.

Celia drew herself up to her full five foot two inches and stuck out her flat chest. Her belly still beat it by a good two inches. "I should have known not to expect any manners or culture from someone who hangs around with the two of you."

"Is that the culture part you're showing me?" I asked. "Because I'm pretty sure it isn't manners."

"Oh, for Christ's sake," Gertie said, "will everyone just be quiet. The reality is, both societies have to work together to pull off the event. This town needs the festival to be a success and the pageant is a big part of that. Fortune is our representative and I expect even the two of you can manage to be polite if you tried really hard."

Pansy looked me up and down, then glanced over at her mother. "She's not as bad as I expected. With Marge being such a manly sort, I thought it would be much worse. She's wearing extensions, but I guess that will have to do."

"At least I'm a natural blonde," I said. "And that's not the only thing on me that's natural." I looked down at her ridiculously large chest.

A flush crept up Pansy's face and she struggled to maintain her cool. "I'm an actress. We're expected to maintain a certain image."

"An actress," I feigned surprise. "No one told me that. I'll have to look you up on Internet Movie Database."

Ida Belle emitted a strangled cry, but before she could let it out completely, Gertie's shoe came right down on her foot.

Pansy's put on a fake smile. "I do mostly industrial work."

"You clean movie sets?" I asked.

"You pedestrian bitch. Industrial acting is usually for private businesses, for internal training and such."

"Oh, like when the library needed a video on the new filing system and the receptionist recorded me explaining it with her cell phone?" I grinned. "What do you know, I'm an actress too."

"Mother," Pansy said, "we've wasted enough time here. The first meeting is tomorrow night. Seven o'clock at the Catholic Church auditorium. Please be on time. I've got my work cut out for me considering the assistance I've been given."

She flounced across the driveway and flopped into her mother's sedan. I figured she'd been standing too long already and her legs were starting to give. Celia shot one last dirty look at all of us and stalked over to her car.

"Remember your running shoes on Sunday!" I yelled.

She slammed her car door, then launched her car back out of my driveway, tires squealing.

"That went well," Ida Belle said.

I shook my head. "You're sure we can't just kill her?"

Both of them were silent for several seconds, then finally Gertie cleared her throat.

"I guess we really shouldn't," she said.

"Hmmm," I stared at the sedan as it screeched around the corner. "Hey, is there a Mr. Celia? I mean, I guess there has to be or Pansy wouldn't exist, but I never hear you say anything about him."

"Maxwell Arceneaux," Gertie said. "A fancy name for such a common man, but he was the only man in Sinful who would put up with Celia."

Ida Belle nodded. "Celia was never nice, but after they married, I'm afraid poor old Max became doormat number one in Sinful. The way she barked at and belittled that man…we always thought one day we'd wake up and hear that he'd smothered her in her sleep or pitched himself into the bayou."

"So what happened?" I asked.

Gertie shrugged. "One day, he simply wasn't here—all his clothes gone from the closet, his truck gone from the garage. That was over twenty years ago, but Celia still refuses to talk about it."

"And no one knows?" I asked. "I find that hard to believe given how people here talk."

"Celia's cousin let out that they divorced, and I'm sure Celia knows what happened to Max after he left Sinful," Ida Belle said, "but my guess is she finds the whole truth too humiliating or too scandalous. Either way, she's never breathed a word about it."

"But he would show up for Pansy's funeral, right?" I mused.

Gertie brightened. "Now, *that* could be very interesting."

Ida Belle nodded. "Remind me to get a new battery for my video camera."

I was just about to suggest we move our meeting inside when I heard a car engine race around the street corner. We all turned to stare as my friend Ally, a waitress at Francine's Café, screeched to a stop at the curb.

I'd met Ally due to my less-than-stellar domestic habits, which led me to eat at Francine's often and well. In fact, despite my busy murder-solving schedule, I'd managed to pack on two pounds in the past five days. Ally had dropped out of college and returned to Sinful to care for her sick mother, but had remained after her mother moved to an assisted living facility in New Orleans. She still wasn't sure what direction she wanted to take with her career.

Right now, she was leaning toward becoming a pastry chef, which had likely been responsible for at least one of my gained pounds. I had no problem being a test monkey when it came to sweets.

Ally jumped out of her car and raced over to us, then took a couple of seconds to catch her breath.

Gertie gripped her arm. "What's wrong?"

She held up one finger, then bent over and took in a deep breath before rising back up to face us. "Good Lord, I'm out of shape. I left my cell phone at home, so couldn't call, and I walked to work this morning. So as soon as my shift ended, I ran home and grabbed my phone, which was dead, of course, as I never remember to charge it, so I jumped in my car and raced over."

I looked over at Gertie and Ida Belle, but they appeared to be as lost as I was.

"So," I said, "the reason for you running yourself into heart attack mode is…"

"Oh, right. Pansy Arceneaux came to town early. I heard all about the pageant and knew Ida Belle and Gertie took you to New Orleans for a day of beauty, but Pansy came early and I wanted to warn you—"

Ally broke off and stared at them, then groaned. "I'm too late. I have got to do a better job with my cell phone."

Gertie patted her arm. "It's okay, dear. We appreciate the effort, especially as it involved running in Louisiana summer heat and humidity."

As I was already feeling sticky from the aforementioned heat and humidity, I waved a hand at the house. "Let's get inside before we all melt."

We all trailed into the kitchen and I poured everyone a glass of iced tea and placed Ally's latest creation—brownies that should be illegal—on the breakfast table. Ida Belle snagged a brownie and bit off a huge chunk, then sighed.

"You have a terrific career ahead," she mumbled, still chewing on the brownie.

Gertie sighed. "Stop talking with your mouth full. I swear, sometimes it's like you've regressed right back to high school."

Ida Belle rolled her eyes. "High school is aiming too high." She looked over at Ally. "Pansy and Celia left right before you arrived."

Ally bit her lip. "Was it terrible? Never mind. Of course it was terrible."

I slid into the chair next to Ally and snagged one of the brownies. At the rate Ida Belle was scarfing hers down, I was afraid they'd all be gone soon.

"I suggested killing her," I said.

For a split second, a hopeful look passed over Ally's face and I grinned.

Then she sighed. "I suppose that wouldn't be polite."

Ida Belle snorted and pieces of brownie shot out her nose. "You've got a great future with the Sinful Ladies Society," she said as she grabbed a napkin for her nose and the table. "Just don't hook up with a man, and let us know when you turn forty."

Ally frowned. "Being as every boy I dated in high school ended up sleeping with Pansy—while I was dating them no less—it's sorta turned me off men for the time being."

Gertie patted her arm. "High school was five years ago, dear."

"I have a vivid memory," Ally said. "And six really good reasons to want to see Pansy Arceneaux run out of Sinful with her tail tucked between her legs. Whatever you guys are up to, I'm in."

I looked over at Ida Belle and Gertie to get their take. Ally wasn't "in" on the real me, and it would take some shuffling to dodge things if she was included, but her job at Francine's also offered advantages of hearing the first line of gossip.

Ida Belle and Gertie glanced at each other in that silent communication mode they'd perfected over decades, then Ida Belle looked over at Ally and nodded.

"You will be an excellent asset," Ida Belle said. "Given your position at the café, you'll hear all the buzz."

Gertie piped in, "And if we need to spread something around ourselves, you're the perfect person to get it started." She clapped her hands. "It's like having a covert radio broadcast."

"I don't suppose Celia ever tells you anything?" Ida Belle asked.

"That's right!" I said. "I had completely forgotten that Celia's your aunt. Wow. That means Pansy is your cousin. And she slept with all your boyfriends? That's a whole other level of lousy."

"Got that right," Ida Belle grumbled.

"Aunt Celia doesn't trust me," Ally said. "She's well aware of Pansy's high school shenanigans but wants to pretend that Pansy is perfect. I tend to remind her that she's not, something Aunt Celia doesn't appreciate."

"Good girl." Gertie nodded.

"I have to admit, it does give me pleasure, but the downside is that Aunt Celia won't be sharing her secrets with me."

"That's okay, dear. Celia's secrets aren't all that

secure. We usually find everything out."

I swallowed a bite of brownie. "Why did Pansy come early? Was that one of Celia's tactics?"

Ally frowned. "I don't think so. They were in the café this morning and I mentioned that I thought Pansy wasn't coming for a couple more days. Celia got that guarded look that she gets when she's hiding something. Pansy said the film she was working on had wrapped up early, so she'd left since she was so anxious to see her mother."

"Horseshit!" Ida Belle exclaimed.

Gertie sighed. "It's not the best of language, but I'm afraid I have to concur."

"Oh, I know she was lying," Ally agreed. "Pansy's a horrible liar and everyone with a clue and the Internet knows she's not getting film work."

"Maybe she committed a crime," Gertie said, "and she came home to hide from the law."

"You've been watching *Law & Order* again, haven't you?" Ida Belle asked.

Ally shook her head. "Pansy's not smart enough to commit a crime and make it ten feet away from the scene, much less thousands of miles. More likely, she slept with the wrong woman's husband and had to get out of town."

I brightened. "Hey, maybe the jilted wife will track her down here and settle up. That would fix everything and none of us would be anywhere near the bullet spray."

"There's something worth praying for," Ida Belle said.

"As much as I'd love to attach a high-society crime to Celia for all of eternity," Gertie said, "the most obvious choice is that Pansy's broke, evicted, or both. She can't possibly have friends, so the only person to run to is mommy Celia."

"If Celia doesn't want us to know, then it could be leverage," I said, my mind already whirling with options. "First order of business—find out why Pansy came home early."

Everyone raised their glass and gave me a single nod.

Brownies in. Brownies out.

Chapter Three

I'd just gotten settled in bed with my laptop when my cell phone rang. I started to let it go to voice mail. I was completely beyond patience for any more emergencies, and as Ida Belle, Gertie, and my CIA partner, Harrison, were the only ones with the number, whoever was calling would likely only serve to aggravate me. Unfortunately, none of those people would call this late unless it was important.

I let out a huge sigh and reached for the phone, then cringed when I saw it was Harrison. This was not going to be pretty.

"What the hell, Redding?" he started in as soon as I answered. "I got a pop last night on Sinful that two people held some old women hostage and were subsequently killed. Do you know anything about that?"

"Maybe a little."

"Please tell me you did not kill those people."

My silence apparently said it all.

"Jesus H. Christ!" Harrison raged. "You'd be less obvious as a Wiccan hooker in Salt Lake City. You can't go around killing people when you're off-grid, especially average citizens."

"Average murdering citizens."

"My alert doesn't say anything about murder."

"Remember the dead guy they found in my yard? The two dead people murdered him. The hostages got too close to the truth, and I had to rescue them."

"Even though it meant blowing your cover? I assume Deputy LeBlanc will be calling today. I'll talk to Director Morrow and see what the backup plan is."

"You won't be getting a call. Deputy LeBlanc doesn't even know I was there."

"So how is he explaining two bodies?"

"The hostages took credit for the kills."

"The hostages? Two little gray-haired ladies?"

I smiled. "I'm not the only person in Sinful who isn't everything I seem."

I gave Harrison a brief rundown of Ida Belle and Gertie's background and told him the story they'd concocted the night before and sold to Deputy LeBlanc.

He was silent for so long, I thought he'd either hung up to call and have me committed or passed out from disbelief. "Unbelievable," he finally managed.

"Yep, but I've seen them in action. They're the real deal."

"How much did you tell them?"

"Only the agency I work for and that I was off-grid with Middle Eastern arms dealers gunning for me."

Harrison sighed. "The more people that know, the higher the risk of exposure."

"Normally I would agree, but this town is a mare's nest of drama that I am not qualified to navigate. I'm safer with them covering for me."

"Morrow is still going to shit."

"Please don't let him pull me out of here."

I hated the slightly pleading tone to my voice, but it must have worked.

"I'll try to pass the report off as overblown, but you have got to keep that town off his radar."

I rolled my eyes. Like I'd had a choice in any of it. "I'll do what I can, and Harrison…thanks."

I hung up and settled back down with my laptop. I had a ton of research to do before that meeting tomorrow night. The day with Genesis had been informative, but it had also highlighted just how vast the field of beauty was and how little I knew. I had to cram or no way would I be able to pull this off. Pansy and Celia were just the type of people to go poking around if they thought something appeared off. I wasn't about to let two nosy, spiteful women blow my cover.

I opened the browser and tried to concentrate on hair and makeup, avoiding all thought about what Morrow was going to say when Harrison told him the watered-down story of what had happened in Sinful.

At five minutes till seven, Ida Belle, Gertie, and I walked inside the Catholic Church and headed down a long hallway toward the GWs' meeting room. I'd spent the last twenty-four hours studying flash cards and reading every Internet article I could find on beauty tips. At two a.m., I'd run out of brownies, but being the team player that she was, Gertie not only answered her phone, but also made another batch and brought them right over. They weren't as good as Ally's, but I wasn't about to complain.

I was high on sugar and coffee and completely lacking sleep and likely, any common sense.

Gertie pointed to a branch in the hallway and we turned right, almost slamming into a woman, probably in her mid-twenties, who was practically jogging toward the exit, her husband a couple of steps behind me. It didn't take a psychologist to see there was trouble in marital paradise.

"I cannot believe you suggested letting that woman get her hands on our daughter," the woman said as she pushed past us. "Why didn't you tell me she was back in town?"

The man shot us an apologetic look before hurrying after his clearly angry wife. "I didn't know she was in town. For Christ's sake, Joanie, I haven't spoken to her since high school."

"Then why did she call your cell this afternoon?"

"I didn't answer so I don't know, and I don't want to know."

The woman pushed open the exit door and continued her charge out in the parking lot.

"What was that about?" I asked, figuring Gertie and Ida Belle had the scoop on everything in town.

Ida Belle shook her head. "Another satisfied customer of Pansy's—the husband, I mean. Mark and Joanie have been a couple since the crib, but Pansy got him drunk one night at a party when Joanie had the flu and the rest is history."

I cringed. "That's horrible."

"She's a horrible person," Gertie said. "I know Pastor Don says everyone can be redeemed, but I have my doubts about that one."

"She'd have to be sorry to be redeemed," Ida Belle pointed out. "And Pansy has never been sorry. In fact, she's taken great pleasure in rubbing it in other women's faces."

I sighed. "Let's get this over with."

Excited voices echoed from the room long before we reached the door, and I frowned as I realized some of them sounded much younger than the average GW age. My worst fears were confirmed when I opened the door and saw that the room was filled with monsters—short monsters, shorter monsters, monsters with big hair and too much makeup, monsters crying, monsters fighting over toys. It was scarier than my last mission in the Middle East.

Pansy spotted me from across the room and gave me a big, fake smile. "Isn't this great," she said, although I'm certain she immediately clued in on the fact that I didn't think it was great at all. "We figured why not do a trial run with some of the contestants."

"Some?" A sliver of horror ran through me. "There's more?"

"Oh yes! Every mother with a child under the age of ten will have her little darling in the pageant."

I glanced around the room, stunned at the sheer volume of little people. As I'd seen only a handful of children during my stay in Sinful, I assumed they were usually caged…or drugged.

"Since I decided to do this last-minute," Pansy went on, "I figured you wouldn't bring supplies, so I set you up at a table with some of mine."

She pointed to a table with more beauty products

than Walmart and I glanced over at Gertie and Ida Belle, whose expressions gave me no doubt this plan wasn't last-minute, as I'd already suspected.

"And you want me to do what? Sell the products?"

Pansy sighed. "Of course not. I want you to make up these girls. You can't expect these children to know anything about fashion. Look at their mothers. Those women are clearly not qualified to apply moisturizer."

Pansy frowned at the mothers, who were huddled in a corner, probably planning their escape. They all looked normal to me, but apparently, if you didn't have fake boobs and tons of hair and makeup, you may as well be a man in Pansy's book.

"Go ahead and get familiar with the products. They're the absolute best, of course—I can't use substandard products on my skin. It's my sales canvas, and must be kept refreshed and new-looking."

"Good thing they're not looking lower," Ida Belle grumbled. "Because the rest of her is used all to hell."

Gertie poked Ida Belle in the ribs with her elbow, but I could see her bottom lip quivering. I didn't bother to hold in my smile. I'd already decided that Ida Belle was who I wanted to be when I grew up—assuming, of course, that no one shot me before then.

"You must be Pansy's co-chair." A man's voice boomed behind me and I turned around to a man with a familiar face strolling toward me. When I realized the face was familiar because I'd seen it on lawn signs, I sighed.

Five foot eleven. Two hundred forty pounds. High blood pressure. Low testosterone. Flat feet and bad knees.

"Mayor Fontleroy," I said and forced myself to maintain the smile and stick out my hand. "It's a pleasure to finally meet you."

Ida Belle coughed and I saw Gertie's elbow dig deeper into her ribs.

He took my hand but didn't shake and didn't speak. Instead, he held it far too long to be remotely appropriate while he looked me up and down.

"The pleasure is most definitely mine," he said finally.

"You're probably right," I said and pulled my hand away from his, with the uncomfortable feeling that he pictured me standing there naked.

Ida Belle coughed again, but this time, Gertie just handed her a tissue. Then she reached back into her purse and handed me a wet wipe, her nose curled as if she'd smelled something foul. It was all I could do not to burst out laughing.

Pansy stepped back up next to me and narrowed her eyes at the mayor, then at me. I suspected with Pansy's choice of tight clothing and huge fake boobs, she had a lot of experience recognizing the mayor's look and behavior.

"I'm sorry to interrupt, Uncle Herbert," Pansy said, not looking the least bit sorry, "but I need to get Sandy-Sue busy with these girls. You want the pageant to be a huge success, don't you?"

Mayor Fontleroy looked over at Pansy and smiled. "Of course, dear. Vanessa is so sorry she couldn't be here, but she had a hair emergency that had to be addressed in New Orleans. I'll let you get on with your business. I'm sure I'll see you around Sinful, Miss Morrow."

Not if I see you first, I thought as he walked away.

Once his back was turned, Pansy snapped her fingers in my face and waved her hand at three little girls, all red-faced and glaring at one another, then me. "This is Kaitlyn, Veronica, and Maude—such an unfortunate name—and they need their makeup and hair done."

Seven years old, sixty pounds each, one missing her front teeth, one with glasses, one with a scar on her elbow—probably an old break. Threat assessment: physically—zero, psychologically—high.

"I'll leave the style decisions to you," Pansy continued, "but I'm thinking glitz—a royal theme. I'd like to raise the class level in Sinful."

"She can do that by leaving town," Ida Belle whispered from behind me.

I gave Pansy a fake smile and a nod, suddenly pleased. I had this one. Half of the articles I'd read last night were on the fashion trends of royals. If there was one thing I knew, it was how a titled woman did her hair and makeup.

I directed my three minions to my corner table and instructed them to take seats. I'd already forgotten their names, so I was henceforth referring to them as Target 1, Target 2, and Target 3.

Target 1's entire face and hands were covered with brownie, so I pointed at Ida Belle. "Get her to the restroom and get her cleaned up. She looks like she fell in dog doo."

Ida Belle grimaced, then pulled the girl's shirt

collar up in the back. "This way, Sloppy."

Target 2 had tangled black hair that looked as if it hadn't been brushed in a century. "Gertie, get to work on her hair. It looks like a haystack."

Gertie picked up the brush and stood behind Target 2, then grabbed a strand of hair, tackling it with a gusto that surprised me and couldn't possibly last for her entire head.

Target 3 had hair that was somewhere in between curly and straight. I looked at the table of beauty products and snagged one of those sticks with two iron plates. I plugged it in and grabbed a brush, but it stuck halfway through her hair and she screamed at the top of her lungs. Everyone in the room stopped what they were doing and turned to stare, except her mother. Her mother stared up at the ceiling, whistling and pretending she hadn't seen a thing.

I took her lack of interest as permission to do the job she'd failed to do. I leaned over and whispered, "Scream like that again, and I'll shave your head."

She stiffened.

"Are we clear?" I asked.

She gave me a stiff nod. *Target acquired.*

I tossed the brush back on the table and grabbed the iron. I'd just flatten it as is, tangles and all. If her mother couldn't be bothered to brush her hair, why should I care? I didn't sign up to parent and last time I checked, I wasn't Jesus. Miracles weren't likely to happen anytime soon.

I grabbed a wad of hair and clamped it in the hot iron, then pulled it out toward me like I'd seen on YouTube. And what do you know, the hair flattened out and looked sorta glossy—as if it had been lacquered. I flipped that piece over her head and started on the one beneath, repeating the process, but this one was wavier and more tangled and came out looking like a bird's nest after a huge storm.

Probably, if I did it slower, the hair would straighten.

I clamped the iron back on the long length of hair and held it there next to her scalp for a second before inching down. As I waited, I glanced over at Gertie who'd just tossed a broken comb on the table to rest with the three she'd already broken off in Jungle Kid's hair.

"Maybe we should cut it?" I suggested. She'd only managed to get one section of the hair untangled and we were going to run out of combs long before she finished.

Gertie studied it for far longer than I expected before sighing and shaking her head. "Neither one of us is qualified."

"That hasn't stopped me from doing half the things I've done since I've been here. Do you know what would happen to me if the other...people I work with could see me now?" I'd barely caught myself before I said "operatives."

Gertie gave me a sympathetic look. "I know this is a bit outside of your norm."

"A bit? That's the understatement of the century. This is ridiculous and what the heck is that smell?"

Gertie looked down and her eyes widened. "The iron," she whispered.

I looked down to see steam coming off the wad of hair I still had clenched in the iron.

Immediately, I released the clip and pulled it away from her head. Unfortunately, the entire bird's nest of hair I'd had stuffed in it came away with the iron.

Chapter Four

"Holy crap!" I clenched the wad of hair and looked at Gertie, alternating between scared and hacked that I was scared over something as stupid as hair. "What do I do?"

She handed me a brush. "Brush that top piece over it. See if it covers."

I lifted the straightened piece that I'd flopped over her head and brushed it back, but no dice. "Her hair is too thin for it to cover."

Gertie felt the stump of burned hair. "This is hard as a rock. It's going to push that straight fine hair out like a tent."

I reached into my pocket. "Is anyone looking?"

"No. What are you going to do?"

"Fix the tent issue." I removed my pocketknife and lifted the straight hair again. Then I started shaving off the hard remnants of burned hair. When it was clear down to the scalp, I let the straight hair fall back down in place.

Gertie leaned over to scrutinize. "It doesn't stick out anymore, but I can see her scalp through that piece."

"Maybe a curly style?"

"It's still too close to the scalp and too thin. The only way you're covering that is with a hat."

I scanned the room, looking for the girl's mother, and finally spotted her in a corner with several other moms, pouring cough syrup into coffee. No threat there.

"Where's Pansy?" I asked.

"Over there." Gertie pointed to a group of girls on the other side of the room. "Why is she teaching them to walk like strippers?"

"At least they'll have a job." I didn't have time to judge Pansy's alternative profession choices. I was in full attack mode.

I grabbed a big barrette off the table and clipped it to a wad of Gertie's victim's hair, making sure I selected a piece from the bottom of the back—at least, I think it was the bottom of the back. Who the hell could tell?

Then I leaned over with my knife and cut the entire clump of hair off her head in one smooth move—like slitting someone's throat. Gertie sucked in a breath and paled a bit.

"Glue gun," I said.

She looked panicked for a minute, then reached for the glue gun on the table behind her and handed it to me. I ran a single strip of hot glue across the edge of the hair peeking out of the barrette, then stuck the whole mess to the bald spot. I had a couple of frightening seconds when I thought the hair was going to come back with my fingers, but I managed to peel them off with the hair firmly glued to her scalp.

I waited the ten seconds for the glue to dry, then flipped the good piece of hair back over and assessed my handiwork.

"It's not bad," Gertie said, clearly impressed. "The color is a perfect match. The only problem is that top piece is untangled and straight and the other never will be."

"I'm going to can the straight hair idea. I'm going to make it big."

"Are you sure...I thought we were going for the royal look."

"I saw a ton of pictures on the Internet of this giant hairdo a royal was wearing. Don't worry. I got this. What about her?" I pointed to Gertie's victim. "Can you cover the damage?"

Gertie rolled her eyes. "It was an improvement."

"Good, then get back to work before Pansy gets back. Maybe you can pull the whole wad back in a ponytail and hide it with bows?"

"That's a great idea and shouldn't take very long."

"Good. My idea for this one will only take a couple of minutes, then I can get on makeup. Where the heck is Ida Belle?"

"You called?" Ida Belle's voice sounded behind me.

I turned around to see Ida Belle still clutching the shirt collar of a now completely soaked girl. "You were supposed to clean her face," I said, "not hose her down like she's going upstate for ten years."

"She wouldn't stand still and I don't have a lot of patience. That's what happens when you ask a bunch of old maids to get involved with children. You get potluck."

She had a point. Most of the Sinful Ladies Society had never been married, therefore, did not have kids. In fact, the more I thought about it all, the more I realized just how far Celia had carried her plan to make them look bad at the festival. She knew they weren't qualified to host a child's beauty pageant. Celia probably thought the only misstep in her calculations was not taking me into account, but then, if she knew the truth about me, she'd probably be celebrating from now until Christmas.

"Fine," I said. "Then dry her and her hair and make it quick. Pansy has already done hair and makeup for all her girls." I pointed to the other side of the room.

"Why is she teaching them to walk like strippers?" Ida Belle asked.

I sighed. Sometimes I swore she and Gertie shared a single train of thought. "Just get on the hair."

I grabbed a wad of hair on my girl and combed it backward at the root, lifting it away from her scalp in a haphazard manner. Then grabbed the next and did it again. Gertie looked over and raised her eyebrows.

"Are you sure about that?" she asked.

"I saw it online. Trust me."

She didn't look convinced, but went back to wrestling her girl's hair into a ponytail. I made quick work of my girl's hair, which now blossomed out from her head in giant puffy waves. It needed color, but I didn't have time to dye it, so I grabbed colored ribbons and attached it with barrettes so that a rainbow of colored ribbons wove around the tangled waves. It would have to do.

Her skin didn't have the pasty white tone I'd seen in the photos, but black eyeliner would still show up on tanned skin. So I grabbed the pencil and went to work. Her eyebrows were already dark, but not big enough or dark enough. I drew a thicker box around them and started coloring. Then a dash of red for the checks, thick red for the lips, and dark gray for the eyes and I was done.

Ida Belle sat down the blow-dryer and frowned at her girl's hair, which now resembled a black haystack. I swear the woman was creating more work. She reached for a brush and I cleared my throat.

"Ida Belle," I interrupted her before she could do more damage. "I saw some party trays when we came in with pepperoni on them. Can you bring one over, please?"

"You want to eat? Now?" She looked over at Gertie, who shrugged.

"Just do it," I said. I didn't have time to explain my genius. Ida Belle would just have to see it along with everyone else. She whirled around and stalked across the room to grab a party tray, then stalked back, grumbling all the way, and shoved it at me, over the girls' heads. I put the tray on the table, grabbed a stack of pepperoni and a stapler and went to work.

Ida Belle's eyes widened and her jaw dropped. For the first time since I'd known her, she was speechless. I smiled. All that worry they'd had over me and a beauty pageant and I was so good I'd scared the words right out of her.

"Oh my God! Stop! What are you doing?" Pansy's frantic, shrill voice sounded behind me.

"I'm making her costume," I said. "Flank steak would be better, but the pepperoni was all I had available."

I looked over at Pansy, whose expression was a mixture of shock and horror. "You're stapling food to her shirt." She put her hand over her mouth. "I'm going to be sick."

The dramatics lasted only a split second, then she shifted from fainting delicacy to flushed and angry. "Are you trying to make a fool of me?"

The entire room went dead silent and turned to look at us. I frowned. I'd expected jealousy and a bit of anger as I'd upstaged her, but I hadn't expected rage. And no doubt about it, Pansy was ready to blow.

"I'm sure you do a fine job of making a fool of yourself," I answered. "I'm just following your instructions. You said it was a royal theme."

Ida Belle and Gertie left their posts at the back of the heads and walked around to see the object of Pansy's rage. Gertie yelped and started fanning herself with a paper plate. Ida Belle covered her mouth with her hand. I couldn't tell if she was horrified, like Pansy, or trying not to laugh, but knowing Ida Belle, I was guessing the latter.

"No one in the royal family," Pansy stammered, bits of spittle flying out at me, "would ever look that way. Not even in private."

"That's where you're wrong," I argued, refusing to give up my ground. "The woman I'm imitating is all over the Internet. Google 'Lady' and she's the first thousand images that pop up."

Gertie emitted a strangled cry and bent over, clutching her stomach. Ida Belle lowered her hand just a bit, and I could see her lower lip trembling.

"Not...," Ida Belle began, "um...not Lady

Gaga?"

"Yeah, that's the one. I've never heard of that family name, but then, I don't exactly run with titled Europeans."

"I'm going to pass out," Gertie said and slumped over in a chair, dropping her head between her knees. I could see her shoulders shaking.

I didn't think it possible, but Pansy's face flushed a deeper shade of red. "You...you philistine! I will not work with someone as stupid as you."

I froze, hoping the forced immobility would prevent me from taking her out right where she stood. That one simple word—*stupid*—thrust me right back to my childhood. I could still hear my father's voice echoing through my head.

If you were a boy, you wouldn't be so stupid.

That was it for me. I'd already taken more than my share of crap over this and it stopped right here.

I leaned over and looked her straight in the eyes. "Call me stupid one more time and you'll be talking with no teeth from here on."

Something in my expression must have gotten to her because she took a step back from me as her mother, Celia, ran up to stand beside her.

"Are you threatening me?" Pansy asked.

"I don't make threats. I make plans."

Apparently, having Celia next to her propped up Pansy's backbone because she lifted her hand and attempted to slap me. Her attempt ended when I grabbed her wrist only centimeters from my face, then twisted it backward until she screamed and doubled over. Celia grabbed my arm, trying to wrestle it off her daughter, but she was no match for my death grip.

"If you ever even think of touching me again," I said, "I'll kill you. In fact, maybe I'll just do it now and save the world the hassle of dealing with you."

I felt something cold, hard, and round press into the small of my back, and Ida Belle leaned over to whisper, "Don't do it."

I was ninety-nine percent sure she was holding me up with a curling iron, but with Ida Belle, there would always be that one percent doubt. I could easily disarm her, but that would draw even more unwanted attention as well as highlight skills I didn't want the rest of Sinful to know I possessed.

I released Pansy and spun around in time to see Ida Belle tossing the curling iron back on the table. She gave me an apologetic look and grabbed her purse.

"I take it we're done here?" Ida Belle asked.

"Oh, you're done here," Celia said, smugly. "You're all done permanently. When Herbert hears about this, he'll remove the SLS from the festival permanently. I'll make sure of it."

"Promise?"

"Thank God!"

Ida Belle and Gertie sounded off at once and I had to grin. "Let's go find something worthwhile to do," I said.

Ida Belle gave Celia and Pansy a big grin. "Already a step ahead of you," she said as she strolled off. Gertie and I hurried after her, none of us saying a word until we climbed into Gertie's ancient Cadillac. Then Gertie and Ida Belle burst into laughter so hard they were crying.

"Is someone going to let me in on the joke?" I

asked, two seconds away from walking home.

Ida Belle let out a gasp and formed some semblance of control. "You really thought Lady Gaga was royalty?"

"I'm guessing she's not?"

Gertie started on round forty-six of laughter as Ida Belle wiped her eyes with her hands and shook her head. "She's a pop star—a huge pop star—with a reputation for outlandish looks. Has a good voice, too."

Gertie nodded. "'Bad Romance' is my jam," she managed to gasp out.

"I have no idea what that means," I said. "So let me get this straight—this Gaga took it upon herself to take on a title even though she's not royalty. And I suppose her look wouldn't be on Pansy's approved list of people to mimic?"

"Probably last on her list ever."

I threw my hands up. "Well, how the hell was I supposed to know people were assigning themselves titles? I was in the Middle East. I don't know what a bunch of Europeans are up to."

Gertie started giggling again, then covered her mouth with her hands when Ida Belle shot her a dirty look.

"Actually," Ida Belle said, "Gaga is American." She tilted her head and stared at me for a couple of seconds. "You really don't know anything about this. I thought for a while you were pulling our leg, but you're not. Don't you own a television…listen to the radio?"

"No and no. The agency has a television in the break room. Thirty minutes is all you need to know what's going on everywhere."

Gertie stopped giggling and lowered her hands. "Then what do you do when you're not working?"

"I don't know," I said. "Learn a new martial art or weapon skill. Go to the gun range. My partner, Harrison, owns a lot of farmland upstate. Sometimes we go up there and blow stuff up—see who can come up with the best explosive..."

I frowned, suddenly realizing just how empty my real life was, especially compared with life here in Sinful. Which was really odd when you thought about it. I'd left a city with over half a million people where I had no life and come to a city of less than three hundred where I'd acquired one in a matter of hours.

Interesting and sad.

Ida Belle and Gertie had gone silent and were both looking at me with something that might be sympathy. It was an expression I rarely saw, so I couldn't be certain. It was also something I didn't want to see again.

"Look, I love my life," I said. "I can't wait to get back to it. It may not seem like much to you, but it's what I know and what I want."

Ida Belle nodded. "We understand. In order to do your job, you almost have to live in a different world than the rest of us. We did it once, and assimilating back here once the war was over was the hardest thing I've ever done."

Gertie rolled her eyes. "You still haven't assimilated," she said to Ida Belle, then looked back at me. "I know this has been difficult for you, trying to fit into this town. Sinful is a strange place by even regular southern standards. It's a whole different universe from what you're used to."

"But you've been doing a fine job, considering," Ida Belle said.

"Hmm." I was pretty sure they were trying to make me feel better, but it had the opposite effect. I had finally realized just how narrow my focus was. How much life was going on in the world that I had zero knowledge of or exposure to.

Maybe that needed to change.

Not that I was going to run out and buy hair products or anything—nothing drastic. But it wouldn't hurt me to read something besides books on weaponry, and I could probably turn on the television in Marge's living room to something besides CNN.

"Ladies," I said, before I could change my mind, "I think it's time I figured out what's going on in the rest of the world outside of politics and war."

Gertie smiled and clapped her hands. "This will be fun."

Ida Belle shook her head and grumbled, "This will take a lifetime, and I'm no spring chicken."

"Do you have to complain about everything?" Gertie asked.

"Only if I'm awake."

"I'll try to make it painless," I said. "I'll only do the fun and interesting stuff."

Ida Belle perked up. "Well, in that case, there's a drag race in Mudbug this Saturday."

Gertie waved a hand in dismissal. "You and your obsession with cars."

"What's a mudbug and why do people drag-race in it?" I asked.

Ida Belle looked over at Gertie and grinned. "Dinner? Francine has boiled crawfish tonight. It can be lesson number one."

"This involves food, right—Francine's food?" I needed to be sure because I was fairly certain the only thing I was up to at the moment was eating or killing something. Eating seemed like the safer option, although this crawfish stuff sounded sketchy.

They both laughed and Gertie put the car in gear and tore out of the parking lot. I took that to mean "yes" and slumped back in my seat, the tension leaving my neck for the first time in the last forty-eight hours.

It seemed my incompetence in the field of beauty had yielded a reprieve on the pageant front. With any luck, I'd be stricken completely from participation and could go back to my seemingly futile attempt to lie low.

One could only hope.

Chapter Five

The next morning, I woke up to a pounding sound and for a minute, I thought it was all in my head—literally. Sinful was dry, but Gertie's enormous purse always contained a couple bottles of Sinful Ladies Society cough syrup, aka their own moonshine brew, and she'd spiked our colas while we plowed through stack after stack of crawfish. Crawfish, as it turned out, didn't look anything like fish, but more like an odd crab. To my surprise, they tasted fantastic, and I'm fairly sure I made a glutton of myself—with the crawfish *and* the moonshine cola.

After we staggered out of Francine's, I spent the next half of the night drinking beer and watching random television, the only interruption being when some drunk called Roscoe called me begging for a ride home from the Swamp Bar. Apparently, his girlfriend, Peggy Gail, had caught him asking a "smokin' hot broad" for her phone number and told him to find another way home. I finally hung up, unable to convince him that I was not his buddy Catfish.

Between the cough syrup and the beer, I'd put

back more alcohol in a single night than I usually did in a month—although I still wasn't as drunk as Roscoe—hence the initial belief that the pounding was the awakening of a world-class hangover. But when I saw the pictures on the exterior wall rattling, I realized it was someone pounding on the front door.

I glanced at the clock, which read six a.m. Seriously? Was I never going to get a good night's sleep in this town?

I threw the covers back and stalked downstairs in my boxers and tank, not even bothering with a robe or shoes. People bang on your door before the chickens are awake, what they see is their own fault. Besides, the only people rude enough to bang that loudly and this early were Celia and Pansy. If I had to kill them, this way I'd have fewer bloody garments to dispose of.

I flung open the door, already hacked and ready for war, but neither Celia nor Pansy was responsible for interrupting my sleep. Instead, Deputy Carter LeBlanc—former Marine—stood on my front porch, looking aggravated as only a gorgeous man could.

On my first day in Sinful, my inherited hound dog, Bones, dug up a human bone in my backyard and put me smack on the good deputy's radar. Ida Belle and Gertie had dragged me into an investigation in the hopes of clearing their friend, Marie, which made Deputy LeBlanc take an even closer look at me. Unfortunately, several of his closer looks involved my being in various states of undress or thin-wet-clothing exposure.

Like now.

He gave my sleepwear one look, then sighed and shook his head. I wondered briefly if it was illegal in Sinful for women to wear boxers, but then, waking me up to see what I was wearing was entrapment. No matter the law, I could work my way out of that one.

The only illegal thing I'd done, that I was aware of, was drink moonshine at Francine's Café, and it was decidedly overkill to harass me about it at six a.m., but I figured I'd just confess, agree to pay some fine, and then get back to bed.

"You caught me," I said. "Can you just give me a fine so that I can go back to bed?"

His eyes widened. "I'm afraid a fine isn't possible in this case."

I threw my hands up. "Then what the heck is the fine for drinking moonshine in a public place— marrying a resident, attending church seven days a week, lynching in the town square?"

In my past run-ins with Deputy LeBlanc, he'd looked almost amused with my sarcastic wit, but no sign of amusement existed now. I frowned. This visit was about something vastly different from being drunk in public.

"Where were you yesterday, starting at seven p.m.?"

I wanted so badly to quiz him before answering, but something in his expression told me now wasn't the time. He was all business, and he wasn't happy about whatever business he'd come here over.

"At seven, I went to the Catholic Church with Ida Belle and Gertie to help with the beauty pageant stuff for festival. We were there about thirty minutes before we were invited to leave."

Deputy LeBlanc nodded. "Did you go home after that?"

"No. That's where the drinking in public part came in. We went to Francine's and ate a ton of crawfish and drank cola spiked with Sinful Ladies Society cough syrup."

Carter closed his eyes for a couple of seconds, and I knew he was mentally counting to ten. "What time did you leave Francine's?"

"About nine o'clock."

"And you came straight home and stayed here?"

Starting to get a little irritated with all the questions and no explanation, my snarky side began to creep out. "Where else is there to go? Everything closes by six except Francine's."

"You were alone?" Carter asked, completely ignoring my tone.

"I didn't pick up one of the senior citizens or any of the married men down at Francine's and haul them home with me, if that's what you're asking. You interested in the spot?"

In the past, Carter had flirted with me when the opportunity had presented itself, but this time, he didn't show any sign of taking the bait. Instead, he just stood there frowning, studying me. My curiosity piqued. Whatever had him up this early and on my doorstep must be bad.

"Are you going to tell me why you're asking these questions?"

"In a minute. According to one of the pageant workers, you got into a fight with Pansy Arceneaux."

"Oh good grief! Is that what this is about? Pansy got her panties in a bunch and you're going to arrest me? I suppose Lady Gaga makeup is illegal in Sinful."

"No. But murder is."

"Murder?" A wave of panic ran through me and I forced myself to remain calm. "But who...not...Pansy?"

Carter nodded. "Celia heard a noise around midnight and went downstairs to check. She found Pansy lying on the kitchen floor, dead."

I stared, waiting for the punch line, but one look at Carter's face and I knew his story was very real. My heart dropped to the bottom of Sinful Bayou. The worst-case scenario had come home to roost. I'd threatened the woman just hours before she was murdered. No way was I ducking out of scrutiny this time.

"How was she killed?"

"We're not releasing that information at this time."

Of course they weren't. Not that it mattered. I'd invented ways to kill people. Sinful couldn't possibly have come up with a technique I couldn't master.

"I don't know what to say. Yes, I got in a fight with Pansy and threatened her, but I didn't mean it. It was just something you say in the heat of the moment when someone's hurling insults at you. Besides, I can't possibly be the only person in Sinful who's threatened Pansy."

"No, but you're the most recent. I'll verify your story with Ida Belle and Gertie, not that I find them particularly trustworthy, but if they can't vouch for you at midnight, it doesn't do you a lot of good."

I felt a flush run up my face. "You can't possibly

think I did this. I've barely been here a week. That's hardly enough time to develop feelings so strong that I start killing people."

"Rationally speaking, you're right, but what I find interesting is that you didn't seem shocked when you found out I was investigating a murder. Most people are squeamish about that sort of thing, especially if they knew the victim. Even if they didn't like them."

I scrambled for a suitable reply. The reality was, one more body didn't really make a big difference in my stats, especially as we were talking about a death I wasn't responsible for. I'd been directly and indirectly associated with more dead people than I could count.

"I guess it hasn't sunk in," I said, but I could tell my poor, pitiful me statement hadn't even made a dent. Time to move to the ego strike. "I can't believe Aunt Marge would bring me down here, knowing how dangerous this place is."

He raised one eyebrow. "Oh, we have our share of deaths. Lots of people here have dangerous jobs and even more take unnecessary chances, but the only murders I've seen since I've been deputy are the two that happened after you showed up in town."

I felt a flush run up my neck. "The first guy was dead long before I got here. I hardly think I sneaked down here years ago, killed a perfect stranger, then came back years later to implicate myself by finding the evidence."

Carter nodded. "True. But the second one wasn't dead until last night, and you were the last person to threaten her."

"That you're aware of." Because I was certain I hadn't killed Pansy, my mind was already whirling with possibilities—a landlord she'd skipped out on, loan sharks, a pimp, anyone forced to listen to her for more than thirty seconds—the possibilities were endless.

"Someone could easily have followed her here from Los Angeles," I pointed out. "Sinful may not be a hotbed of criminal activity, but LA certainly is. Maybe someone should see how Pansy was supporting herself while she was out there, because it only takes minutes for anyone with an Internet connection to find out she wasn't making it acting. Not any kind of acting she wanted to claim, anyway."

He narrowed his eyes at me, and I could tell that one, he didn't like my assessment, and two, it was something he'd already thought of himself.

"You," he said and pointed his finger at me, "will not get involved in this investigation. Playing cop almost got Ida Belle and Gertie killed last week. Next time, it could be you, or all three of you."

I smiled. "But if *I* killed her, I wouldn't be in any danger if I attempted to investigate, so the fact that you've told me to stay out of your case also tells me you don't think I did it."

"Doesn't matter what I think. It only matters what I can prove, and unfortunately, I can't prove you *didn't* do it. That may be all that the good citizens of Sinful need to rally behind Celia and demand your arrest. Remember, Pansy was the mayor's niece. This could get very ugly."

Holy shit!

A jolt of fear shot through me like a lightning

bolt. I'd completely forgotten to put things in perspective. I wasn't back in DC, with hundreds of thousands of people and a staff of attorneys at my disposal. I was an outsider in a small bayou town who'd just threatened a dead, politically connected local.

So much for flying below radar. I'd just blown the whole thing up.

❦

After an admonition from Carter not to leave town, I flew upstairs to call Harrison and ensure that my Sandy-Sue cover was shored up from every angle possible. I felt my lower back tighten as I clenched the phone, waiting for him to answer. He was not going to be happy about this turn of events, and Director Morrow was going to flip.

"What's wrong?" Harrison sounded half-asleep and half-stressed, well aware that a six a.m. call on a line reserved only for emergencies couldn't be a good thing.

I gave him a brief rundown of the situation, leaving out the details about the actual reason for the fight. His responses went from chuckling at my foray into the beauty world to disbelief over the fact that yet another body had racked up on my watch.

"Jesus, Redding!" he said when I'd finished. "You can handle the most complicated weaponry like you designed it yourself and traverse some of the world's deadliest terrain like it's a stroll in the park, but you can't manage to lay low in some hick town for even a day without landing smack in the middle of trouble. I'm beginning to think Morrow is right and *you're* the real problem."

I clenched my teeth and struggled not to tell him

off. It wasn't totally his fault. You had to actually *be* in Sinful to figure out it was a whole different level of strange.

"This town is the most difficult assignment I've ever had," I said. "I'm not trained to be a civilian, and I'm certainly not trained to host beauty pageants. How well would you do in my place?"

"I'm a guy."

"Exactly my point. And for all intents and purposes, so am I, at least from the average female perspective. I am just as lost here as you would be. It's like Alice in Wonderland. This place is not anything I know or can draw a comparison to from my normal life. What the hell kind of assassin would I be if I was worried about messing up my hair or breaking a nail?"

He sighed. "Okay, so it's definitely not the best cover for you, and I'm sure Morrow had no idea that you'd be thrust into the limelight with all your feminine shortcomings up for exposure. But this makes four bodies since you've been there."

"What can I do about that when they keep popping up? I can't keep people from being murdered by someone else."

"Shit." Harrison was silent for several seconds, and I knew he was at as much of a loss as I was. "If you hadn't threatened her, this might not be as serious. What did she do, anyway?"

"She called me stupid."

"Oh."

Harrison knew better than anyone how that one word could set me off. People could call me crazy, ugly, emotionally stunted...even fat, although that would be a lie. But no one called me stupid or weak and got away with it.

"And what did you do to get her to that point?" he asked.

Crap. I'd been hoping he wouldn't work around to the details.

"I didn't do the kid's makeup to her standards."

"No big surprise there, but a lousy makeup job rarely incites name-calling. What kind of makeup did you do—zombie apocalypse?"

I sighed. "Lady Gaga."

"You didn't."

"She said it was a royal theme. How was I supposed to know that some pop singer is masquerading as royalty?"

"I don't know whether to laugh or cry. Do me a favor, Redding. Open up the curtains on the front of that house so that everyone can see in. Then sit in front of the television and watch anything but CNN for a good twelve hours. You can catch up on what the rest of the world is in on and have witnesses that you were at home in case another dead person turns up."

I'd already spent half my night dedicated to learning pop culture, but I saw no reason to admit that to Harrison. "What are you going to tell Morrow?"

"As little as I can get away with, and even that is likely to send him into cardiac arrest."

"He can't pull me out. It would only make things worse."

"I know. That's the part he's going to like the least. You know how he hates having no options."

"Join the party."

"Hang in there, Redding. I'll do what I can on

this end to ensure your cover remains intact. I'll get back to you when I have information. You stay in plain sight as much as possible. Sit on the corner of Main Street and play the banjo if you have to. But try to have witnesses just in case this beauty queen wasn't the only one whose number is up."

I hung up the phone and walked into the bathroom, my knotted back and neck in desperate need of a hot shower. In reality, I hadn't been alone often since I'd been in Sinful, but I suspected that Ida Belle and Gertie, with all their shenanigans, weren't the best of alibis. I hated to drag any of the other residents into my crap, but if I did everything in public, then I supposed that would leave everyone I interacted with off Carter's hit list.

I grabbed a handful of hair extensions and clipped them in a wad to the top of my head. It was things like showering that had me longing for my one-inch locks trapped beneath all that fake hair and glue. Some of the long strands escaped my grasp and I grabbed more barrettes to hold them in place.

The entire process could have been simplified if I'd just use the mirror, but I hadn't been able to look at myself since we'd returned from New Orleans two days ago. Genesis was a genius, no doubt about that. She'd exposed the delicate bone structure of my face while leaving me looking like I was hardly wearing any makeup at all. The simple, casual look she'd given my hair was no fuss and would be easy for even me to keep up.

Then she'd spun me around in that chair to see her handiwork in all its glory, and I'd been struck speechless. Genesis, Ida Belle, and Gertie had taken it as my stunned appreciation for Genesis' extraordinary abilities, but that wasn't it at all. What had rendered me speechless is that I looked exactly like my mother. Ever since I'd arrived in Sinful—freshly made over to look completely different from my normal self—I'd caught glimpses of her in me. A pitch of the eyebrow, a curve of the lips, but they'd been flashes.

Like seeing something out of the corner of your eye.

And I'd made sure I didn't linger in front of the mirror, allowing the whole view to come into focus. But when I'd seen myself in that beauty shop mirror, it was as if I were looking at a photograph—my favorite photograph of my mother. She was sitting in a lawn chair on the beach at Martha's Vineyard. We were on family vacation, the last one before she died. Back then, my father was a different man—human even.

Entire years of my adult life ran together and disappeared into the nothingness of my mind, but I could remember every minute of that summer at the beach. It was absolutely perfect.

Then she'd died. And nothing had ever been right again.

Chapter Six

I'd barely gotten the coffee on before I heard the second set of a.m. pounding on my front door. This time, Ida Belle and Gertie stood on my porch, looking a bit worse for the wear. Ida Belle was in her usual morning-interrupted wear of robe and curlers. Gertie, who'd attempted to dress, had on a purple sweat suit and a giant red headband pulling her unkempt hair off her bloodred face. She was leaning against the doorjamb and wheezing like an asthmatic.

I peered around her but didn't see Gertie's ancient Cadillac parked nearby.

"Did you run over here?"

"*Someone's* car is out of commission," Ida Belle said, who surprisingly didn't even seem winded.

"And *someone* won't take her car out when it's foggy lest it mar the perfect detail job," Gertie wheezed.

"Your car was fine last night," I said. "What happened?"

Gertie sucked in a deep breath and her expression shifted to that look she gets when she doesn't want to admit to something. "I hit a squirrel on the way home from Francine's."

I stared. "Sooooooo? Does Sinful have giant elephant squirrels made of titanium or something?"

Ida Belle waved a hand and walked past me into the house. "The damn squirrel was in a tree."

"Not wearing your glasses again?" I asked.

"I don't need glasses!" Gertie protested.

"Uh-huh," I said and motioned her inside. "Can you get to the kitchen without breaking the living room furniture?"

"Smart alecks," Gertie said as she stalked by. "Both of you."

"How come you're not winded?" I asked Ida Belle. She'd had to jog to my house the week before and had been huffing like a train.

"I didn't let myself go as much as Gertie, but that run last week let me know how lazy I've been. I'm doing two miles a day on my treadmill. Since I was in reasonably good shape before—unlike some people—my body has responded quickly."

As we walked single-file toward the kitchen, Gertie gave Ida Belle's back the finger.

"I saw that," Ida Belle said, without so much as even a slight turn of her head.

I grinned and followed them into the kitchen, where Ida Belle grabbed the coffeepot. Gertie breath was almost restored, and I gave her outfit another assessment.

"Red Hat Society meets *Jersey Shore*?" I asked.

Gertie stopped stirring her coffee. "What?"

I waved a hand at her. "The look. I thought it was a mash-up. Never mind."

Ida Belle raised her eyebrows. "What exactly did you *do* after we left Francine's?"

"I can tell you what I didn't do—I didn't kill Pansy Arceneaux."

Ida Belle nodded. "We know."

"Poor Celia," Gertie said and sniffed.

"Yeah," I agreed. "You're not supposed to outlive your kids, much less find them murdered. I bet she's a mess."

"Beatrice tells us they had to sedate her. One of Celia's cousins came to get her and took her to New Orleans."

Silently, we all took a seat at the kitchen table. By unspoken agreement, no one spoke for the first few sips, then Ida Belle sighed.

"While I've enjoyed a whole two minutes completely free from Gertie's babble, we have a serious crisis on our hands."

"I know," I said. "I've already reported in to my partner at the agency. He's going to do everything he can to shore up my cover on his end, but if Carter digs too deep, it won't hold."

Gertie's eyes widened. "Surely, he doesn't think you did this. Carter is young and not yet up to our standards of stealth and subterfuge, but he's smart."

"Gertie's right," Ida Belle said. "You have opportunity and ability, but you really don't have motive. No one will take that beauty pageant stuff seriously as a reason to kill someone."

"People in Sinful might," I said.

Gertie's eyes widened.

Ida Belle blew out a breath. "Crap. You're right. No one in Sinful could stand Pansy, but they won't be willing to admit that one of our own killed her. You're the easiest scapegoat, and that falling-out last night will only cement it in the majority of their feeble minds."

"Not to mention," Gertie said, "that our idiot mayor will be looking to find a quick solution. It's an election year. Hard to get votes if you're letting the people who murder your family members get away."

I'd already known it was serious, but hearing them spell out all the details made it sound all that more bleak. "So what do we do? Harrison told me to stay in public as much as possible—that way if anyone else turned up dead, I'd have an alibi."

"That's fine if we assume another murder victim is forthcoming, and in the same manner Pansy was murdered," Gertie said. "But what if it was an isolated incident?"

Ida Belle shook her head. "And it probably was. Let's face it, Pansy was the type of person who created long-term grudges. You heard that argument between Mark and Joanie last night at the church."

"That's true," Gertie said. "It's entirely possible someone has been waiting all these years for her to return to Sinful so that they could exact their revenge over something from high school."

I frowned. "You really think someone could have waited all these years to kill Pansy over some high school slight? That seems a bit far-fetched to me, even by Sinful standards."

Gertie's brow creased with the effort of her thoughts. "Maybe thinking about getting revenge all these years drove them steadily over the precipice of sanity. What started as a simple revenge plot morphed into murder."

I stared. "Really, Dr. Phil?"

"Did you spend all night watching television?"

Ida Belle asked.

"No. Well, half, but it was a very informative half."

Ida Belle rolled her eyes. "Oh yeah. The Red Hat Society, those fools on *Jersey Shore*, and Dr. Phil have all the answers."

"Probably more answers than you got waxing your car."

"For your information, I had a season marathon of *Justified* when I got home."

"Oh!" Gertie's eyes widened. "That Raylan Givens is so hot he almost makes my television melt. You would like him, Fortune. He's always killing people."

"But it's all justified," Ida Belle said. "Get it?"

I stared at them, as confused as ever. "There's a show on killing people? I thought only the federal government could sanction that sort of thing, and they usually don't want anyone knowing about it. I'm not sure I could work with a film crew following me around."

Ida Belle looked upward with her prayer face. "It's not a reality show. It's fiction. Like a novel but on television."

"And he *is* a federal marshal," Gertie pointed out.

"That explains everything," I said. "Those marshals are loose cannons."

"Ha!" Ida Belle laughed. "Said the spook."

"This hot, gun-slinging marshal sounds really interesting," I said, "but it doesn't help with our current situation. As long as Pansy's murderer is unidentified, I'm going to be a suspect. I'm sure you're right that Carter is no fool, but he doesn't have as much at stake as me."

Gertie nodded. "And he has to follow the law and all sorts of other rules in order to investigate."

"But we don't," Ida Belle said.

"Exactly." Gertie smiled.

A small trickle of excitement went through me, followed by a larger trickle of fear. "I don't know. Look what happened last time we got in the middle of a murder investigation."

"Yes, let's look at that," Ida Belle agreed. "Our friend was exonerated, two bad guys died, and we all found out just how much our friends cared about us and us for them. Horrible, awful things."

"And we got to see Fortune in action," Gertie added. "That was better than *Justified*, even though she's not my type."

"You forgot about the trip to the island of stink," I said, "my having an extension ripped out of my head and retrieved by Rambo Rottweiler, almost getting shot at the Swamp Bar, and Deputy LeBlanc catching me in far too many states of partial to pretty-much-full undress. You two might have been entertained, but I was mostly horrified."

Ida Belle frowned. "There is that. But you have to weigh it against the other risk—that Carter will conduct a very careful and deliberate investigation, but it won't move as quickly as we would. I don't have to tell you that the faster this whole nightmare is put to rest, the better your chances of maintaining cover."

I sighed. As much as I hated to admit it, she was right. But the mere thought of launching into Nancy Drew mode with the two seniors of doom was definitely not what I'd had in mind, especially only days after I'd barely escaped with my life and cover. My dignity was long gone and not even worth mentioning at this point, which I guess could be seen as a positive. Depending on how you looked at the situation, I had one less thing to lose.

"I guess it wouldn't hurt to look into a few things." I pointed my finger at them. "But…no islands of stink, no redneck bars, no trespassing at Deputy LeBlanc's house, and no riding naked in cars."

Ida Belle grinned. "Well, if you're going to take all the fun out of it…"

"That's exactly what I want to do. You two can find some other form of entertainment. My humiliation level is maxed out, and I thought it had reached its peak before I arrived here. Besides, Deputy LeBlanc already told me straight-out to leave this alone. He'll be watching me for more reasons than one."

"Well, he can't spend all day and night watching you *and* conduct an investigation," Ida Belle pointed out. "We'll have to make sure we know where he is at all times so we can choose the best opportunities to do our own investigating."

"Sinful doesn't have any more law enforcement?"

"Just Sheriff Lee."

I waved a hand in dismissal. Sheriff Robert E. Lee was a hundred if he was a day, and still rode a horse everywhere. The horse was also a hundred.

"Where do we start?" I asked.

Gertie perked up. "I think we should make a list of everyone in Sinful, then eliminate them one at a time as we determine they couldn't have done it."

"That's a great idea," I said, "except for the part where according to Deputy LeBlanc's questions, I gather Pansy was murdered around midnight. That means most people would be at home. We can hardly go asking every household to alibi themselves. Not only will it get back to Carter, but no one can be certain that another person was in bed sleeping if *they* were in bed sleeping."

"Then we should eliminate them based on method," Gertie said.

I nodded. "Definitely a better way as it takes into account ability, but there's one big problem—I don't know how she was killed. Deputy LeBlanc didn't say and I'm sure that's deliberate. All he said was Celia found her dead on the kitchen floor."

"How she died must have been obvious," Ida Belle pointed out, "for Carter to leap straight to murder."

"Gunshot seems the most likely," I said, "but Celia—and most of her neighbors—would have heard it. Unless they used a silencer."

Ida Belle frowned. "There's no need for a silencer unless you're killing a person. I doubt many people in Sinful have them."

"We don't need *many* people," I pointed out. "We just need one who hated Pansy."

Gertie shook her head. "Fortune's right. The first thing we've got to do is find out how she was killed. That information alone could eliminate a third of the town."

"If someone in Sinful killed her, that would help," I said, "but I still think we need to find out what Pansy has been up to all these years in California."

"I agree," Ida Belle said, "but we're going to have to be careful. Carter will be following that angle as well. People are sure to mention it to him if they're questioned twice."

I nodded. "So we'll be careful. We won't ask questions that seem like they're because of her death. I bet we can still find out quite a bit. At least give us an idea of what kind of person Pansy is as an adult. I know how she was before she left, but she could have developed dangerous habits in LA."

"True," Ida Belle agreed.

"But first things first," I said. "I assume the Sinful grapevine has been hobbled as far as information goes, and I'm going to guess that Carter already told Celia to stay quiet about everything. Will she?"

Gertie and Ida Belle looked at each other, in their silent communication mode, then both looked back at me and nodded.

"If it were about anyone else," Gertie said, "she'd have gone door-to-door like a Jehovah's Witness, flapping more than clotheslined sheets in a hurricane, but she was always tight-lipped when it came to Pansy's escapades."

Ida Belle snorted. "That's because most of Pansy's escapades included being naked with someone else's boyfriend. Not exactly the reputation Celia wants reflecting on her parenting skills, or lack thereof."

"Maybe we should make a list of everyone Pansy slept with," I suggested. "Then track back to angry girlfriends."

"That's easy," Gertie said. "It's the same list as the Sinful residents—just remove the women and the men past a certain age range. At least, I think we should remove the women."

I waved a hand in dismissal, certain Gertie was exaggerating Pansy's alley cat ways on some level, but not certain I wanted to know the true extent of her sexual reach on one cup of coffee. "Back to the task at hand. How do we find out how Pansy was killed?"

Ida Belle and Gertie looked at each other and I could tell before Ida Belle opened her mouth that I wasn't going to like the answer.

"The only way is to see Carter's files on the case."

"Doesn't one of your partners in crime work at the sheriff's department?"

Ida Belle nodded. "That's how we found out so quickly. Myrtle used to work night dispatch, but there wasn't much call for the position except drunk and disorderlies, so they made her the admin last Friday. Carter called her in to work early today."

"She learned how to text without looking at her phone, so she sent us a message as soon as she knew what was up," Gertie added.

"So have her hack Carter's computer like she did before."

"He's changed the password," Gertie said. "We think maybe he caught on that we were siphoning off police information during the whole Marie debacle."

I blew out a breath. Carter was right, of course, that Myrtle had hacked his computer and given us confidential information, but it was frustrating that he'd caught on so quickly and moved to act.

"I don't suppose you know anything about

computers?" Gertie asked.

"Only what normal people know. The agency has an entire department dedicated to working with computer stuff. I've worked with them on most of my missions. Those people are on a whole different plane of existence."

Ida Belle cocked her head to the side. "There might be someone—"

"Oh no!" Gertie shook her head so hard her headband slipped over her eyes.

"What?" I looked back and forth between Ida Belle and Gertie, who were locked in a stare-down.

"Give me another option then," Ida Belle challenged.

"I...we can...crap." Gertie sighed. "But I want to go on record saying that even though I can't think of a better idea, I think this is a really bad one."

"I'm almost afraid to ask," I said. "Should I ask?"

"She wants us to see the sorcerer," Gertie said.

I looked back and forth between them, waiting for the punch line, but none was forthcoming. "Wow. I thought I had heard some ridiculous crap since I've been here—most of it from you two—but this takes it all. You want to have some voodoo person tell us how Pansy was killed? Why don't we sacrifice a chicken while we're there?"

"The Sorcerer is not a voodoo priest. He's a techno-anarchist," Ida Belle said.

Gertie nodded. "He's rumored to be a member of Anonymous."

Somewhere in the back of my mind, a tiny bit of recall flickered. "Those people who hack major computer networks? We had a meeting about them at the agency."

"Exactly my point," Gertie said. "If the CIA held a meeting about them, then they're dangerous. I don't think it's a good idea to get involved with those people."

Ida Belle waved a hand in dismissal. "Those are only rumors. No one knows for sure that he's in that silly group."

"No one knows for sure he's not, either," Gertie insisted. "In fact, all we know about him is rumor. Some say he makes his money in the stock market, but others say he's laundering money for Colombian drug dealers. Some say he's got a set of mercenaries complete with assault weapons and man-eating dogs guarding his residence."

"We're customers," Ida Belle argued. "You don't kill your customers."

"I don't know," I said, getting a bad feeling about the entire thing. "If he can afford mercenaries, why would he help us? We can't pay him a lot of money."

"No, we can't," Ida Belle agreed, "but if he's truly an anarchist that means the chance to best a law enforcement agency should get his attention, especially in the interest of justice to the common man. And I think you have something he'd be interested in for trade."

"Me? I came here with a suitcase of clothes that I'd never even worn and a laptop. I seriously doubt he's interested in my substandard computer equipment or girlie clothes. Heck, I'm not even interested in the girlie clothes."

"Not you, directly, but Marge. According to the grapevine, The Sorcerer has a collection of historical military weaponry. Before her death, Marge accumulated quite a collection herself."

I blew out a breath. I knew all about Marge's collection. I'd accidentally tripped the sliding wall in the back of her closet and had practically drooled at the wall of beautiful weaponry hidden behind the panel. And Ida Belle was right: Some of it was old, but in excellent condition—the kind of items historical collectors would pay top dollar for.

But there was only one problem.

"Nothing in this house belongs to me," I said. "It belongs to the real Sandy-Sue."

"Based on what I know about Sandy-Sue," Ida Belle said, "she wouldn't have anything to do with weapons. And no one is aware of Marge's collection except the three of us."

"It's still stealing," I said.

Gertie shook her head. "Normally, I would agree, but if Marge were here, she'd give you a gun. I have no doubt about that."

Ida Belle nodded. "And you are doing all Sandy-Sue's work, cataloging the estate for sale—for no pay. Surely, that's a fair trade."

"Well, I haven't exactly done anything about cataloging."

"You have all summer for that," Ida Belle said, "and Gertie and I will help."

"It's a fair trade," Gertie said.

I stared out the window at the muddy bayou that cut across the backyard and weighed all the options. I didn't like appropriating Sandy-Sue's property, but I could probably get the agency to pay her back for the cost of the gun when this whole thing was over. The thing that bothered me the most was the many unknowns surrounding this Sorcerer. For all we knew, he could be part of the intelligence community himself, or even worse, someone who made his living trading information to the wrong people. If he was dialed into the arms community, there was a chance he knew about the price on my head.

"We need this information," I said finally, "and if we move forward with this Sorcerer thing, I want to be there to get a read on him. But I have a concern." I told them about my fear of an arms community connection.

"Which would be a completely valid concern if you remotely resembled the way you described your appearance before coming to Sinful, but unless he has facial recognition software, I doubt he'd recognize you all 'girled' up."

"Actually, I was 'girled' up during the failed mission, so any pictures would be of me then. I had a handler for the girl end of things," I explained.

"What did you look like for the mission?" Gertie asked.

"I had waist-length brown hair and brown contacts. I also had these fake teeth things that gave me a slight gap in the front and this horrid bra that shoved my boobs under my chin. I had a cleavage cleft the size of most people's butt crack."

"What kind of clothes did you wear?" Ida Belle asked.

"Tight and clingy. Would have shown every ounce of extra fat if I'd had any. And the most ridiculous shoes—like balancing on stilts—but they make a good weapon in a pinch."

Gertie raised her eyebrows. "Were you supposed

to be a prostitute? No, don't answer that. The less we know about your real life, the better."

"Probably true," Ida Belle said, "although the shoes-as-a-weapon thing is intriguing. Anyway, it sounds like you looked completely different than now. Throw on one of those Ellie May sundresses and a pair of sandals and pull your hair into a ponytail like you always do and you'll look like any other hometown girl."

I mulled it over for a moment, but couldn't find a flaw in Ida Belle's assessment. "Okay, so it's a plan. Do you know where this Sorcerer lives?"

Ida Belle nodded. "According to my intel, he lives in Mudbug. It's about an hour from here."

I narrowed my eyes at her. "Your intel?"

Gertie shook her head. "A kid she plays *Call of Duty* with says one of their regular group is The Sorcerer."

Finally, a pop culture item I was familiar with. I'd played *Call of Duty* at Harrison's place on many occasions. "And you think this kid knows what he's talking about?"

Ida Belle shrugged. "I'll put an online call for a meet with this regular. If he doesn't turn out to be capable of what we want, the only thing we've lost is time and a tank of gas."

"All right," I said and rose from the table. "Then I guess we're going to see if The Sorcerer can work some magic. I'll go upstairs and become a girl. You two figure out how we're going to get to Mudbug, since Gertie wrecked her car and I refuse to ride in the Corvette with all Ida Belle's rules."

Gertie jumped up, looking perky. "I got an idea about that while we were jogging over."

Ida Belle rose from her seat, looking as skeptical as I felt, but it was their job to work it out. "I'll be ready in fifteen minutes. How long will it take for you to fix the car?"

"Oh, only five minutes or so," Gertie said, "but it will take me the other ten, at least, to jog back to my house."

"You have got to start working out," Ida Belle said as they headed down the hall.

"I work out."

"Knitting is not a workout."

Chapter Seven

I was still grinning when I ran upstairs to change. The front door banged shut as I flipped through the sparse selection of girl clothes hanging in my closet. Finally, I pulled a white sundress with pink roses on it out of the closet. It looked like the item least likely for me to wear either as myself or as my prior undercover persona.

My hair was in reasonably good shape, so I pulled it back in a ponytail as Ida Belle had suggested and plugged in the curling iron. While I was waiting on the curling iron to heat up, I put on some moisturizer and a bit of lip gloss. Despite my considerable dexterity under normal circumstances—normal for me, anyway—I still hadn't mastered putting on the eye stuff without poking myself in the eye, so I left it off.

I flipped the ends of my ponytail around the curling iron, making sure I didn't leave it on long enough to burn the hair off. Who knew those things got that hot? I took one final look in the mirror before slipping on some pink sandals, then snagged a pistol from Marge's secret stash, careful to avert my eyes from the full-length mirror in her bedroom.

I was afraid my appearance would nauseate me, and I really needed to eat breakfast. When you agreed to escapades with Ida Belle and Gertie, you never knew what you might get. It was always best to maintain your energy level at its peak.

I was just finishing scrambled eggs when I heard Gertie's Cadillac pull in my drive. At least, the engine sounded like Gertie's Cadillac, but an odd clinking sound accompanied it now that I hadn't heard before. I tossed my dishes in the sink, grabbed my purse, and headed out the door.

Then stopped and stared.

One glance was all I needed to put the clinking sound into perspective. The front bumper, which previously could have charitably been referred to as mildly serviceable, was now a rolling eyesore. It was mangled and dented and popped forward on each end of the car. Bright pink and green duct tape held the whole thing in place. All hope that we could make this trip unobserved went straight out the window.

"Stop gawking and get in," Ida Belle yelled from the passenger's window.

Despite the hundreds of really good reasons this was a bad idea, I walked down the sidewalk and hopped in the car. Gertie took off down the street, the bumper flapping in the wind.

"Wouldn't it have been better to pull the bumper off?" I asked.

"It's wedged stuck in the middle," Ida Belle explained. "I couldn't pull it out and Gertie couldn't find her crowbar."

"At least I got the squirrel out of the grill," Gertie said.

Ida Belle nodded. "Dinner at my house tonight."

I grimaced. It was definitely a Hungry Man night for me.

The drive to Mudbug seemed to comprise one long stretch of the same piece of marsh, but we passed the time by speculating on the Pansy situation and Ida Belle and Gertie arguing over the last season of *American Idol*. Since I'd been rousted out of bed too early, I spent the arguing time dozing until Ida Belle poked me and said we were there. I propped myself upright and took my first look at the town.

Mudbug looked very similar to Sinful, only slightly bigger. It had one main street with worn brick buildings and the same southern charm, and I wondered how many of these tiny towns with bayous, banana pudding wars, and deadly wildlife Louisiana contained. Then I wondered how many of them had an abnormally high percentage of murders given the population.

At the corner of Main Street stood a statue of a frumpy older woman, but what caught my attention was the added extra that someone had placed on the gray plaster.

"Who is that woman in the statue?" I asked.

Ida Belle looked over at the statue. "Some rich woman who died and left the town property."

"Why is she wearing a cone bra?" I asked, particularly pleased with myself for recognizing it from a music video I'd seen last night.

Ida Belle waved a hand in dismissal. "Probably kids."

At the end of Main Street, Gertie turned and followed a winding road that ran parallel to a bayou.

Houses were larger than those I'd seen closer to town and spaced farther apart. Finally, Gertie swung into a driveway and followed the circular drive up to the front of the house.

"Are you sure this is the place?" I asked, looking out at the large plantation-style home sitting on a well-manicured acre of land.

Ida Belle checked her phone and nodded. "This is the address he gave me."

"I don't see any snipers or killer dogs," Gertie said.

"If you saw them," I pointed out, "they wouldn't be snipers."

"It doesn't look scary at all," Gertie said.

"In my experience," I said, "that's usually the worst case, but this time, I suspect someone's playing a joke on Ida Belle." I climbed out of the car. "Let's get this over with."

We walked up the sidewalk to the front door and I pressed the doorbell, somewhat relieved when no sounds of killer dogs were forthcoming. After several seconds, I pressed the bell again.

The door flew open and I looked straight down a hall and into a living room. Then I adjusted my gaze down...way down.

Male—maybe ten years old, four feet six, seventy pounds soaking wet, skin that had never seen sunlight, which was rather a frightening contrast to his black hair and blue eyes.

"May I help you?" he asked politely.

"Yes," I said. "We're here to see, um...The Sorcerer?" I barely kept myself from cringing at how stupid that statement sounded. Why hadn't Ida Belle gotten a real name? It had never occurred to me that a techno-anarchist might have a normal life, complete with wife and kids.

He studied us for several seconds, then his gaze settled on Ida Belle. "Are you Killing Machine 1962?"

"Yes," Ida Belle said.

He stuck his hand out. "I'm The Sorcerer."

I tried to control my surprise as Ida Belle shook his hand, not quite managing to hide her own amazement. How in the world had she not clued in to the fact that her gaming buddy was younger than her wardrobe? More importantly, how had this scrawny, pasty child managed to convince intelligent adults that he was some kind of cyber vigilante?

"Aren't you just adorable?" Gertie said, beaming at The Sorcerer.

I frowned. Maybe the "intelligent" part of my question was the problem.

"This are my friends, Gertie and Fortune," Ida Belle said.

"A pleasure to meet you," The Sorcerer said and motioned us inside.

We followed him down the long hallway and through the living room, where an older man and woman sat watching television. They never even glanced over at us, but from the thin frames and pale white skin, I figured they had to be his parents.

He veered off down a hallway to the left and then through a door on the right with a sign hanging on the front of it that read CLIENT MEETING—DO NOT DISTURB.

"Sometimes, my parents forget I'm working," The Sorcerer explained, and pointed to a huge ornate desk and chairs in the middle of the room. I slid into a chair between Ida Belle and Gertie, discreetly casing the room. Bookcases ran along every wall, completely circling the room, and every square inch of them was filled with books. I looked at some of the titles—*Combinatorics*, *Brain and Cognitive Sciences*, *Nonparametric Statistics*, *Macroeconomics*, *Advanced Japanese*. Yikes.

The Sorcerer took a seat behind the desk and pressed a remote. A panel of bookcases on our left side slid back, revealing four enormous flat-screen televisions, forming a large rectangle on the wall. One of them flashed with New York Stock Exchange information. The others contained market information for different countries. Apparently, the stock market rumors had been accurate. Hopefully, the "money laundering for drug dealers" rumors were stories created to keep people away.

"Your parents don't mind you doing business in the house?" I asked.

"Why would they?" he answered. "It's my house."

All righty then. His parents were probably afraid of him. Heck, for that matter, I was a little afraid of him myself.

"You said you had a law enforcement problem," he said, getting down to business.

Ida Belle nodded. "My friend Fortune got into a silly argument with an obnoxious woman last night and might have threatened to kill her. All in the heat of the moment, you understand. She wasn't serious."

Because I'd been sort of serious, I forced my innocent face. I'd worn it so many times in Director

Morrow's office that I'd perfected it.

"I assume this obnoxious woman is now deceased?" The Sorcerer asked, not appearing the least bit concerned with the subject matter.

Ida Belle nodded. "She was murdered last night around midnight. Fortune is a visitor in Sinful, and the obnoxious woman is the mayor's niece—"

"And you're afraid she'll be railroaded," he interrupted. "Probably accurate, given the circumstances and small-town mentality, which I am all too familiar with. So what do you want from me?"

"We think the sheriff's department needs some help getting things right, but of course, they would never allow us to take part in the investigation."

"So you're going vigilante to try to solve the murder and get your friend off the hook." He studied me for a moment, then gave Ida Belle a nod. "That's admirable, and although I'm skeptical about your potential success, I'm happy to help. You brought the item?"

Ida Belle nodded at me and I pulled the gun from my purse and handed it to him across the desk. For the first time since I'd laid eyes on him, I saw a flicker of emotion. He liked the offering.

"You were right," he said to Ida Belle. "The gun is pristine and well worth the exchange."

He opened a laptop, typed something in, and then two of the giant televisions shifted to blank Internet search screens. "What information do you need?"

I held my breath. This was the breaking point. So far, I hadn't seen any evidence that this kid was willing to break the law, but we were about to find out just how much he liked the gun and/or disliked the government.

"We'd like to know the case details," Ida Belle said. "Specifically, how she was killed, but any additional information is appreciated."

He nodded and started tapping on the keyboard. The screens whirled with a series of numbers, scrolling so quickly I could barely tell what they were, much less assign any meaning to them, but apparently all of it made sense to The Sorcerer. Suddenly, the scrolling stopped and the monitor revealed the Sinful Sheriff's Department's file server.

"You're good," I said, unable to keep my appreciation to myself.

The Sorcerer gave me a "no shit" look, then asked, "Name of the victim?"

Ida Belle gave him the name and he tapped again then frowned.

"A record has been created for the victim," he said, "but it doesn't contain any information. Official results from labs and the coroner won't be available right away, of course, but the attending officer should have made notes. Let me check something else."

He tapped again and the sheriff's email appeared. A paltry list of email appeared containing subscriptions to hunting magazines and one highly disturbing reminder to refill a Viagra prescription.

"I take it the sheriff isn't leading the investigation?" he asked.

"The sheriff is older than dirt and couldn't lead turtles without being run over by them," I said. "Deputy LeBlanc is leading the investigation."

He tapped again and pulled up Carter's email. We all leaned forward as he clicked to open an email to the coroner, then sat back in disgust over what we'd read.

"Interesting," The Sorcerer said. "It appears your deputy is smarter than the average small-town guy. He's electing to keep the entire file in writing until the case is solved. He's directed everyone to send reports by courier only." He looked over at Ida Belle. "Does he have a reason to suspect the sheriff department's system has been compromised?"

Ida Belle squirmed a bit in her chair. "We might have a friend who works as an admin, and she might have known the deputy's password and used it a time or two."

The Sorcerer smiled. "We are kindred spirits, Killing Machine, but in the future, you should leave specialties to the specialists, then you can remain undetected."

Ida Belle sighed. "How was I supposed to know things would get this out of hand? Usually nothing happens in that town."

He nodded and tapped some more on the keyboard. Then he scribbled some numbers on a piece of paper and handed it to Ida Belle. "I figure you're not going to let this go. That code will get you past the sheriff's department's security system."

Gertie's eyes widened with a bit of fear, but not enough for my taste. Ida Belle happily tucked the numbers in her purse. I could see already that it was going to be a long ride home, fighting all the way.

"Let me do one more thing before you go," The Sorcerer said and tapped in Pansy's name in some complicated-looking search engine. The screen flashed and pulled up a single entry—Pansy's Facebook page.

The Sorcerer opened the Facebook page, scanned it, then blanched. "No wonder someone killed her." He flipped back to the search engine and pointed at the screen. "Notice I can only find one Internet mention of your victim."

"Does that mean anything?" I asked.

He nodded. "There are only two kinds of people who don't have an Internet presence—those who intentionally keep their identity from online sources and those who don't really matter. Given that your victim has a Facebook page where she has posted over five thousand pictures of herself, I'm going to guess she falls in the second group."

I frowned. "She mattered so much to someone that they killed her."

He smiled. "Ironic, yes? She wanted nothing more than fame and attention, and in death, she got both."

He closed the laptop and handed the gun back across the desk, a wistful look on his face. "As much as I'd like to have the weapon for my collection, I can't accept it for work I could not complete. But if you have need of my services in the future, I'd be willing to trade again."

I would have let him keep the gun just to see him work, but I understood his professional code.

"Have you ever thought about doing work for the government or military or both?" I asked, thinking that between me and this kid, we could probably solve most of the world's problems.

He waved a hand in dismissal. "I don't work

with amateurs."

Chapter Eight

"So what now?" I asked.

We were all back at my house, sitting at the kitchen table and eating a plate of Gertie's famous chocolate chip cookies, apparently a "requirement" for Ida Belle if she needed to think. If we didn't solve this murder soon, I was going to need to buy bigger pants, which was alarming if you considered that most of what I had contained stretchy waists.

"We need more information on Pansy," Ida Belle said.

"Aren't we going to break into the sheriff's department tonight?" Gertie asked.

Ida Belle shook her head. "When I talked to Walter earlier he said Carter had been by to stock up on coffee and NoDoz. He's pulling an all-nighter."

Walter was the owner of the General Store and Carter's uncle, and had been in love with Ida Belle for longer than I'd been alive. She'd already turned down so many of his marriage proposals that I wasn't exactly sure why they were still on speaking terms. I suppose I had to give him points for either temerity or plain stupidity. I was hoping for temerity, as I'd liked Walter from the instant I met him.

"I've got nothing, ladies," I said. "The Internet is a blank and we can't go asking Celia what the body looked like when she found it or who hated her daughter enough to kill her, but without even knowing where Pansy lived in LA, we can't start poking around into what might have gotten her killed. I don't suppose there's anyone else in Sinful who might know what Pansy's been up to since she left town, is there?"

Gertie shook her head. "Maybe someone in Celia's crew, but they wouldn't talk to us."

"*And* it would get right back to Carter that we were poking around," Ida Belle said.

"Okay, let's look at the other angle," I said, refusing to be defeated. "If Pansy wasn't followed here by an enemy from LA, then someone in Sinful is the murderer. That means they've been holding a grudge for a lot of years. Surely, you've got some ideas on that."

Gertie gave me an apologetic look. "I'm afraid not. Pansy's shenanigans were all of the teenage type. We tend not to pay much attention to that stuff. I mean, we knew she got around, but I don't know which girls she pissed off in the process."

I perked up. "I bet Ally knows."

"Probably," Ida Belle agreed, "but we have to be very careful getting her involved. Ally and Celia may not be close, but they're still family. Everyone will be watching Ally to see which side of this she stands on."

I sighed. "And they won't appreciate it if it's my side. I get it." The last thing I wanted to do was cause trouble for Ally with Sinful residents. She had to live here after I was gone.

The doorbell rang and we all looked at each other.

"You expecting someone?" Ida Belle asked.

"Who would I be expecting?" I headed to the front door, praying that it wasn't Deputy LeBlanc, there to arrest me.

I was pleasantly surprised to see Marie and Bones standing on my doorstep. I smiled and let them in the house. The real Sandy-Sue had inherited Bones, her late Aunt Marge's ancient hound dog, along with the house and everything in it. My first day in Sinful, Bones dug up a leg bone that belonged to Marie's missing husband, and everything went downhill from there. Marie was one of Marge's best friends, the chief suspect in the murder of her husband, and she promptly went missing.

Ida Belle and Gertie roped me in to helping them find Marie and clear her name, and almost got themselves killed and me exposed in the process. Once the real killers were revealed, Marie's name was cleared, and since Bones knew Marie and loved her, I let her take the old hound to live with her.

"Did he walk all the way over here from your house?" I asked as Bones shuffled down the hall and into the kitchen. He sat in front of the cabinet that contained dog treats and I poured him a couple on the floor as Marie greeted Ida Belle and Gertie.

"He's been quite perky lately," Marie said. "I've had to fence my petunias to keep him from digging."

A trickle of fear ran through me. "There's

not…under the petunias…"

Marie laughed. "No. I'm quite certain the petunias are not hiding any body parts. I made the bed myself last year and pulled out about three feet of topsoil."

I nodded, but still wasn't convinced. When I buried someone, I always went deeper than three feet, and Bones got his name and reputation from being able to find bones several feet under dirt and even water. But as long as the fence was keeping Bones at bay, I wasn't saying a word. The last thing Sinful needed was another questionable corpse.

"Do you want some coffee?" I asked Marie as she took a seat at the table.

"No, thank you. I can't stay for long."

I nodded. "It's probably a good idea for you to avoid us for a while."

Marie brightened. "So you are investigating?" She clapped her hands. "When I heard the whole story down at Francine's, I just knew you wouldn't let this town railroad Fortune like they tried to do me. That's why I'm here."

She reached inside the front of her ruffled blouse and pulled out a large envelope, folded in half. "Best I can figure, this was delivered to my house over a week ago. With everything that was going on then, I hadn't taken the time to go through the mail until today, and I found this."

She pushed the envelope across the table to Ida Belle. Ida Belle looked down at the mailing address and her eyes widened.

"This is from Pansy to Celia," Ida Belle said.

"Why would Celia's mail come to your house?" I asked.

Ida Belle snorted. "Because Postman Bob is a drunk and Marie lives next door to Celia."

Gertie frowned at Ida Belle. "It's not really polite to call him a drunk when you're his supplier. Postman Bob is our biggest customer for cough syrup," Gertie explained.

"Should we open it?" I asked. "It *is* a federal offense to open someone else's mail."

Ida Belle ripped open the envelope and pulled out some papers. "We've got bigger things to worry about than the feds."

"Well, what is it?" Gertie said, leaning across the table to look at the papers.

"It's a note from Pansy," Ida Belle said.

Mom,

Here is the paperwork we talked about. I have to turn it in two weeks from now or the whole deal will be void. I've talked to an attorney, but I have to give him five thousand in retainer before he'll even start working on my case.

I know you don't have much, but I don't have anyone else to ask.

Pansy

Ida Belle flipped the note over and looked at the attached paperwork. "It's an IRS agreement for paying back taxes. Holy crap, Pansy owes the IRS over eighty thousand dollars for federal taxes and more for self-employment."

"Has she never paid in her life?" I asked.

Ida Belle shook her head. "It's all for one year—two years ago."

"How much do you have to make to mount up

eighty grand in taxes in a single year?" I asked.

"A little under two hundred thousand," Marie said, "depending on her allowed deductions."

We all stared at Marie.

"What?" she asked. "I like numbers. I filed all Harvey's business returns as well as our personal."

"I'm storing that away for future reference," Ida Belle said. "It's certain to come in handy at some point."

"Okay," I said, "so what was she doing to generate that kind of income in a single year? I don't believe for a minute that making corporate videos about sexual harassment and computer security pays that kind of cash."

"I agree, it seems highly unlikely," Ida Belle said.

"Can I see?" Marie asked.

Ida Belle handed her the IRS forms. As she scanned them, a blush started at the base of her neck and crept up her face. Finally, she covered her mouth with her hand.

"Is something wrong?" I asked.

"It's all self-employment income that she owes the taxes for. See here?" She showed us a six-digit number on one of the forms. "This is the business code for 'All other personal services.'"

"That doesn't sound like acting," I said.

"No, the description the IRS included is 'sale of leisure services.'"

"Whoot!" Ida Belle said and slammed a hand on the table. "Pansy was a prostitute."

"Seriously?" I asked. "Is that true?"

Marie nodded. "It's definitely possible. The IRS doesn't have a code specific for prostitution, but this is one of the recommended ways of reporting such income."

Just when I thought I'd heard everything. "There are recommended tax procedures for prostitutes?"

"Sure," Marie said. "How else could the IRS get them for tax evasion? I mean, your average streetwalker probably earns well beneath the poverty level, so they wouldn't be worth pursuing even for the self-employment portion. But a high-class call girl can make more than a corporate executive."

I narrowed my eyes at Marie. "Who are you again? And how do you know so much about prostitutes?"

Marie laughed nervously. "I read a lot of sociology studies...and watch television shows about that sort of thing."

"Uh-huh. Well, Marie's somewhat questionable knowledge of the world of prostitution aside," I said, "would Pansy be considered 'high class'?"

"I think that just means she uses a hotel for business and isn't a crack addict," Gertie said.

"Actually," Marie said, "it refers to the clientele."

"So men who pay a lot of money for sex are high class?" Gertie shook her head. "That doesn't sound right, either."

Ida Belle waved a hand in dismissal. "All social commentary aside, the fact remains that Pansy was likely doing something questionable for money, owed the IRS a ton for it, and wanted to see an attorney about it."

"She probably wanted to contest the amount," Marie said. "People in the sex trade don't exactly issue invoices or keep accounting records, so the IRS would have imputed her income based on her lifestyle."

"What's imputed?" I asked.

"Made an educated guess based on her house, car, spending habits…that sort of thing."

"So Pansy was living the high life in LA and got pinched for it by the IRS," I summarized. "This is highly entertaining, but is it relevant?"

"It could be," Ida Belle said and leaned across the table. "We all know Pansy has a habit of going after men who are already taken. What if she slept with them, then blackmailed them to keep quiet about it?"

"Pansy always did take the easy way out," Gertie said. "It would be just like her to figure out a way to get paid long after services were rendered."

I sighed. "We really need to find out what Pansy was up to in California."

"At least now we have an address," Ida Belle pointed out. "We can start there."

"I'll grab my laptop," I said and jumped up from the table.

Marie rose with me. "I'm going to head back. Carter's got the state police guarding Celia's house and I don't want anyone to catch on that I was meeting with you guys."

Ida Belle nodded. "That's smart. You keep an eye out from your house and let us know if you see anything that might help. And thanks for the paperwork."

"And the tax knowledge," I said as I followed her and Bones to the front door. "You're amazing, Marie. You should think about opening your own tax service."

She blushed and gave me a shy smile. "No one's ever given me such compliments before. Thank you." She leaned over to kiss my cheek, then hurried out of the house, urging Bones to pick up his pace.

I watched her walk away before hurrying upstairs, thinking about how Marie and I had more in common than I'd originally thought.

⌒⌒⌒

It was close to midnight before I crawled into bed. I'd been running on sugar, coffee, adrenaline, and sheer stubbornness for almost three days straight, but I needed to get some sleep if I was going to remain at optimum performance, something I would really need tomorrow night. Unless Carter decided to pull another all-nighter, we were going to break into the sheriff's department and find out what was in Pansy's file.

The documents Marie had delivered added new theories to what might have happened to Pansy, but didn't offer anything concrete. What we really needed to make that angle work was a list of her customers, but I had no idea how to get one. We'd easily located the condo she'd lived in—a rental that ran almost seven thousand a month—but a quick search of public records showed she'd been evicted just before arriving in Sinful.

Either her customer list had run low or the one or more who'd been picking up the tab had cut her off. My guess was an angry wife or two was involved. It wasn't much but at least it gave us the real reason Pansy had run home to her mother. Gertie was going to call the landlord on Monday, pretending to be a bill collector, and see if she could get anything out of him.

It was beyond tempting to have Harrison use the agency's many resources to get to the bottom of Pansy's California past, but no way could he get the information he wanted without throwing "CIA" into the requests, and that was sure to get back to Carter as he conducted his own investigation. If Carter found out the CIA was investigating Pansy, he was certain to ask why. That "why" would likely go straight to Director Morrow, who would pull me out of Sinful so fast it would seem as if a hurricane had blown through.

I looked over at the noise-canceling headphones on my nightstand, deliberating whether or not to put them on. Despite all claims that living closer to nature was supposed to be peaceful and good for the soul, I found that the strange noises of the bayou creatures kept me up most of the night. Especially the frogs. The frogs in Sinful sounded like they were attempting opera every night—in Italian. I hated opera. I didn't know any Italians, so the jury was still out on that one.

I sighed and turned off the lamp. It probably wasn't a good idea to put on the headphones considering a murderer was running loose. What if it had nothing to do with Pansy and was just some crazy who hated beauty queens? I would totally understand the sentiment, but given that I was posing as an ex-beauty queen, that put me next in line.

I flopped back on my pillows and closed my eyes, surprised that all I could hear was the gentle flow of the bayou.

Croak.

I sighed and pulled the pillow over my head. Maybe I should consider getting a dog while I was here. I'd had Bones, but he was almost deaf and couldn't even make it up the stairs to warn me of an intruder, much less take one down.

Then I heard the sound of an outboard motor coming down the bayou. It was moving slowly, barely above an idle, but the low rumble carried across the water and into my sensitive ears. At first, I thought nothing of it. Ida Belle had already told me that the middle of the night was often the best time to fish, but when the motor shut off right in front of my house, I sat up, listening for the sound of a restart.

Several seconds of silence passed. Complete silence, as even the frogs had ceased their performance. I jumped out of bed and hurried to the bedroom across the hall to peer out the window into the backyard.

The light from the back porch barely reached halfway across the yard, leaving only patchy moonlight to illuminate the bayou. Dark clouds rolled across the sky, blocking out the sliver of light that had been there before, casting the bank into pitch black. I scanned the edge of the bayou, trying to make out any movement in the inky dark. At first, I saw nothing, then at the end of the yard where a row of enormous bushes that Gertie had called azalea stood, I saw the flicker of a tiny light.

Someone was hiding in my bushes with a penlight.

Chapter Nine

I grabbed my nine millimeter and hurried downstairs and out the front door. Staying close to the side of the house, I crept around to the back and peered into the darkness, trying to locate another flicker from the penlight. To normal people, the wait would have seemed like a long time, but my body automatically shifted into professional mode. My breathing slowed, my senses sharpened, my eyes adjusted to the darkness, and time seemed to stop.

The hunt always felt the same.

The faint rustle of leaves tickled my eardrum and I immediately locked into the location where the noise had originated. A second later, the penlight flashed against the ground before disappearing again in the brush. They were working their way up the side of my lawn, staying just inside the edge of the bushes to do it.

I slipped away from the wall of the house and moved silently across the back lawn, careful to remain hidden in the shadows. I was only five feet away from the figure when they turned off the light and stepped out of the bushes.

It would have been so simple to take them out right then—in fact, it would have been so easy, it seemed unfair. Certainly, no one had a valid reason for sneaking up on my house in the dead of night, but on the flip side of things, the last thing I needed was another body to add to the count. And if I killed them, then I had no chance of finding out what they were up to.

Plan of action decided, I took two silent steps behind them and placed my nine at the back of their head.

"Move and I'll blow you away," I whispered.

"Fortune?" a panicked, female voice responded.

"Ally?" I dropped my gun and spun her around to be sure. She stared back at me, her eyes round as saucers.

"What the hell are you doing?" I asked. "I could have shot you."

Her body slumped and for a moment, I thought she would pass out. Instead, she bent over and took in a huge breath, then slowly blew it out. When she rose back up, she seemed a little steadier.

"Can we get inside?" she asked. "I don't want anyone to see me."

"Yeah, I sorta got that part given that it's past midnight and you didn't ring the doorbell," I said and motioned her to the back door. "I came out the front door. Wait here until I turn off the porch light, then come in the back door."

I hurried around to the front door, scanning my neighbors' houses as I slipped inside. No blinds snapped back into place, but that didn't mean someone wasn't watching. If Ally didn't want to be seen, then this was the smartest route to take. If my neighbors wanted to think I was some strange woman who stalked around at midnight wearing boxers, then they were welcome to those opinions.

Of course, wearing boxers outside at midnight was probably illegal in Sinful, but that was something I'd deal with if the time came.

I flipped off the back porch light and unlocked the door. A couple of seconds later, Ally crept inside. As soon as the door was closed, I flipped on the kitchen light. She lifted her hand over her head, blocking her eyes from the bright light and blinking to clear her vision. My vision took about a second to adjust, and I guided her to a chair at the breakfast table.

"Do you want something to drink—coffee, maybe?" I couldn't imagine what had sent Ally creeping through my hedges at midnight, but I imagined it was something more important than a simple conversation could handle. Otherwise, she would have just called.

She looked up at me, still blinking. "Coffee would be great. I don't think I'll be sleeping for a while—like maybe a week. You scared any thought of rest completely out of me. Good God, Fortune, where did you learn to sneak up on people like that? I never heard a thing and I'm a decent hunter."

I shrugged, trying to play down my skill set. "It's the single-woman-living-in-the-city curse. For a long time, I was afraid to leave my apartment after dark, but winters up north are long and don't provide a lot of light. I realized I was missing out on a good portion of my life, so I took those classes— you know, self-defense and stuff."

Ally shook her head, clearly impressed. "I took a

class when I lived in New Orleans—same reason except for the cold part—but they never taught us anything like you're capable of."

"We had a retired Special Forces guy teaching our class. He probably went a little overboard for the average civilian, but I found his instruction so fascinating that I took private lessons for a couple of years. It was something to do."

That part, at least, wasn't completely a lie. Much of my training had been at the hand of one of the best Special Forces officers the military had ever seen. And I had taken the lessons off of company time and payroll. But he wasn't retired. He was still active.

Boy, was he active.

Training and other things that I'd participated in with Army Ranger Sullivan were some of my fondest rookie memories. I'd found someone with the same interests, the same career objectives, and who had no desire for a picket fence, golden retriever sort of life. Unfortunately, he'd been sent on a mission six months after we met. It was his last.

He was the first person I'd grieved for since my mother. I hadn't been in love with him—we hadn't known each long enough for something that serious—but I think I could have gotten there. Maybe. I don't know.

And I never would.

I pushed thoughts of Sullivan aside and focused on the current situation as I took a seat across from Ally. The color was returning to her face, but she still looked worried. I assumed the worry was in place before I scared her half to death.

"The coffee will take a couple of minutes," I said, "but maybe you should tell me what has you out creeping around lawns at midnight. Is your cell phone dead again?"

"No, but I was afraid to use it. Mr. Walker, who lives next door to me, is a CB radio buff. He has a huge tower in his yard. A couple of cell phone conversations that I thought were private, ended up public knowledge. I suspect he listens to everyone within range. And I cut the home phone off when mother went to the nursing home. No use paying for something I wasn't using."

I stiffened a bit, then forced myself to seem relaxed. "Your house is four blocks from here, right?" If someone in Sinful could overhear my conversations with Harrison, we were going to have to ditch the emergency phones and stick to email only.

"Yeah," she said. "Why?"

"Oh, I was just thinking that Ida Belle and Gertie should probably watch what they say on the cell. You know how they're always up to something."

"Oh, they know about Mr. Walker. That's why they're usually vague unless they're standing in front of you."

"Well, I wish they would have told me that. I could have blown their cover."

Ally laughed. "I'm not even going to ask what cover you could have blown. My guess is they've been avoiding Mr. Walker for so long that they forgot to tell you about him. Plus, I don't think his tower reaches more than a hundred feet or so. Only people on his block are at risk."

I got up to serve us some coffee, then sat back

down. "So what is it that you couldn't say on the phone?"

"Mayor Fontleroy and his wife, Vanessa, had dinner at Francine's tonight. A couple of Celia's friends stopped by to talk to them, and when I heard your name, I moved as close as I could without being obvious."

"I take it the conversation wasn't complimentary."

"They want the mayor to force Carter to arrest you. They said everyone in Sinful knows you did it and that if Carter doesn't move quickly, then he should be fired for incompetence and never allowed to run for sheriff."

I sighed. We'd expected as much, but the locals were moving even faster than I'd thought. "What did the mayor say?"

"He tried to calm them down—said it had only been a day, and they needed to give Carter a chance to correctly do his job or the whole thing could be thrown out in court. But Vanessa was a different story. She agreed with Celia's friends and said she wouldn't feel safe in Sinful as long as you were wandering loose."

I rolled my eyes.

"I know," Ally said. "She's a total bitch, and she's his second wife—the one he traded in his older wife in on. She's a good fifteen years younger than him."

"Let me guess—Celia's sister was wife number one."

"Yep, so the mayor is always trying to smooth things over for Celia because he doesn't want drama. Celia's sister left town as soon as she collected her settlement. Hasn't stepped foot in Sinful ever since."

I frowned, considering all the complications this presented. "Does the mayor pay much attention to the new wife or is she strictly for appearances?"

Ally sighed. "He's a fool. I think he was infatuated with her at first. So much so that he didn't get her to sign a prenuptial, and I know his attorney desperately wanted one."

"Does he have money?"

"A bit of family money, but not as much anymore since his first wife got half when she divorced him—still less than what she should have earned for being married to him, mind you."

"So if this one goes, she'll take half of what he has left."

Ally nodded. "Which can't be much, at this point, because she spends money like she's printing it. It's not like Sinful pays huge salaries, even for the mayor."

"To sum it up, you're afraid the trophy wife is going to put pressure on the mayor to put pressure on Carter."

"And Aunt Celia. As soon as she gets back, she'll be on a rampage. The mayor won't get a moment of peace until someone is arrested, and all indications are that the person they want arrested is you."

"I figured it would get around to this, eventually, but I think we were all hoping for a little more time."

Ally brightened. "So you are investigating yourself? Good!"

"No, nothing like that," I scrambled to cover.

"I'm hardly qualified for that kind of thing."

"I don't know—you strike me as quite observant, and I'd hate to meet you in a dark alley. Besides, you've got Ida Belle and Gertie to help, and they're nobody's fools. I don't believe for a minute that the situation with Marie was resolved by chance. I'd bet a year's salary that the three of you were right in the thick of it."

I was torn. Ally was one of the only people I actually felt guilty lying to, but I didn't want to get her involved, either. Finally, I decided that partial truth was probably the best policy.

"Look," I said, "I'm not going to lie to you and say we're just sitting around waiting for this town to railroad me, but the truth is, I don't want to get you involved. You have to live in this town once I'm gone. What if someone had seen you tonight? Or worse, what if I'd shot you? I don't think that would have helped my case any."

Ally blew out a breath and slumped back in her chair. "I know you're right, but man, it pisses me off."

"You can't afford to appear as if you're on the wrong side of this, Ally. Especially since Pansy is your cousin."

"But the three of you are looking into things, right?"

"Yes. We are following up on several leads."

"I want to help." She held up her hand before I could argue. "No one has to know. In fact, I can probably get more information if the lynch mob thinks I'm siding with them. I can collect information and report it back to you."

I hesitated before answering. My conscience told

me to say no and insist she stay far away from me until this entire mess was over, but my mind said she could be an asset, and we weren't all that flush with assets.

"You promise to be careful?" I asked.

"I promise," she said. "Starting with no more midnight boat runs. If I need to tell you something again, I'll drive somewhere else and call."

"Good. And no trying to get information out of people. Just listen and report. I don't want anyone to get suspicious."

She didn't look completely happy with the request, but I believe she saw the merit in it. "Fine. No questions. I'm a voice-activated recorder and that's it. So have you figured anything out yet?"

"Nothing beyond speculation." I gave her a brief rundown of the IRS situation, not explaining how we got the information, and told her some of our ideas about how Pansy might have accumulated such a tax bill.

Ally's eyes widened. "Wow. Even I didn't see that one coming. I mean, I'd totally believe Pansy was working the sex trade, but it's hard to fathom men paying that much for her."

I nodded. "Especially once you've met her."

"So what are you going to do now?"

"Try and track down her landlord and see if we can find out more about the eviction. Maybe he'll be angry enough to give up something we can use. But beyond that, we don't have much to work on. What would really be helpful is if we knew the names of her biggest clients. I figure there's got to be an angry wife or two in the lot."

"Bet on it." Ally drummed her fingers on the

table, her brow scrunched in concentration. "I bet Pansy kept a list. She's both stupid and vain enough to think it would be okay. She used to keep a notebook with a list of all the boys she slept with in high school. Even rated them on stamina and performance. Two extra points were awarded if they had a girlfriend at the time. Three if they were married."

I shook my head. "It's a wonder no one has killed her before now."

"Tell me about it." She frowned. "If Pansy was evicted, where is all her stuff?"

I shrugged. "It might have been confiscated during the eviction. Or if she was smart, she moved it to storage somewhere. Or she may have sold everything figuring she was coming back home. Why? Do you think the list would be with her things?"

Ally was silent for several seconds, then slowly shook her head. "No. I think she would have brought it with her. A reminder of what she had accomplished. Her own little ego boost."

I nodded. "That sounds likely given what you've told me about her, but Carter probably took anything like that as evidence. If she had a list and brought it with her, it's locked up in the sheriff's department with all the other evidence."

I didn't let on that tomorrow night, I planned to be inside the sheriff's department, poking through that evidence. But at least I knew to look for a list in any of the personal items Carter recovered.

"No, it's not!" Ally jumped up from the table and clutched my shoulders, a huge smile on her face. "Pansy knew Celia was a snoop. She would have hidden the list and I know exactly where she would have hidden it."

I felt my pulse tick up a notch and a swell of hope rose in me. "Where?"

"Under a loose floorboard in her closet. That's where she kept her diary and her sex-rating book."

"Oh," I said, as the hope slipped away. "The house is being guarded by the state police while Celia is away. But even if she were here, Celia wouldn't allow me in her house, much less Pansy's bedroom. I can't imagine she'd let Ida Belle or Gertie past the front door, either, since they've taken up with me."

"No," Ally agreed. "But she'll let me in. I'm family."

"Family she doesn't particularly like or trust," I pointed out.

"True, but Celia would never go against southern manners. When there's a death, family is required to show up and help. Celia won't tell me to go away because I'd only be doing what manners and bloodline call for. As soon as she returns to Sinful, I'll pay her a visit and offer to help her clean her house, cook meals...maybe even choose an outfit for Pansy for the funeral. Even though she won't like it, she won't tell me no."

I smiled up at Ally, that feeling of hope swelling back up. If Pansy had a list, and if she'd brought it with her, and if Ally could get hold of it, we might have a list of suspects.

It was a whole lot of "ifs," but I'd take it.

෴

Despite the fact that I'd been up a good portion of the night, I was too wired to sleep late. I sprang out of bed at six a.m., ready to take on Sinful...until I remembered it was Sunday. That meant a long, unnecessarily boring sermon and that I had to wear a dress. This whole dress-wearing thing was getting to be a habit, and it wasn't one I appreciated. Last night, I'd found myself drooling over a new line of combat boots I'd found on the Internet.

Since I was awake so early, and had eaten way too many dessert items the past week, I decided to take a morning run. Exercising served the dual purpose of keeping me from getting fat as a barn and allowing me to create a mental layout of the neighborhood. I'd looked up the pertinent addresses on Google Maps last night but wanted to commit them to live visual.

I took a good hour for the run, which required me circling the neighborhood at least ten times. I had to admit to losing count after six. Gertie had told me that a lot of people lived on rarely traveled farm roads outside of the cluster that was the Sinful township, but all of the key players in my life resided in the single neighborhood that extended north of downtown.

After the run, I made some notes on layout, street conditions, hedges and other useful hiding places, and the houses that contained dogs—at least, the houses where they bothered to bark. I avoided actually running on Celia's street, figuring I didn't need to give people anything else to use against me, but I was able to get a good layout of the street from the next block.

Once the notes were done and hidden away, I did a load of laundry, cooked and ate breakfast, and was made up and dressed when Gertie stepped onto my front porch at eight a.m.

Gertie jumped back in surprise when I opened the door before she even knocked.

"You're up…and dressed."

"I've been up for hours. And I figured as long as I'm here church is sort of mandatory, but today, probably even more so."

Gertie nodded. "Celia came home last night. The funeral will be sometime this coming week, but they'll probably light candles for Pansy today at service."

"So…no tennis shoes?" My second day in Sinful had been a Sunday, where I'd learned that the first group representative to arrive at Francine's Café after church let out had control of the limited banana pudding supply offered only on Sundays. I'd been cajoled into donning tennis shoes during final prayer and sprinting down Main Street so that the Sinful Ladies could command top seating and dessert privileges. Celia was the sprinter for the GWs, but even with new Nikes, didn't stand a chance against me.

"I suppose it wouldn't be decent," Gertie said finally, looking so disappointed I had to laugh.

"Don't worry," I said and clapped her on the back. "The summer has plenty of Sundays left, and I doubt Francine is going to stop making banana pudding. If I ran today, it might cause a conflict worse than Vietnam."

"You're right. I suppose the least we can do is let Celia step first into Francine's today after church."

"That, and find out who killed her daughter."

"Count on it," Gertie said. "You ready, then? I'd like to talk to Ida Belle before choir practice starts."

"I'm as ready as I'm getting."

Chapter Ten

I'd expected church to be a somber affair, and it was. Sure, the Sinful Baptists and Catholics had their own mini Holy War going on, but murder tended to put superficial things on hold. The preacher started off with a Bible passage, then launched into his sermon on the responsibilities of Christians as far as kindness goes.

I listened for a bit, then my mind wandered back to our investigation, where it stayed until Gertie elbowed me to stand for the final prayer.

Even though the Sinful Ladies had called a temporary cease-fire in the Banana Pudding War, Gertie and I had taken seats at the back of the church, so we were the first outside. The Catholics were still in church, so we crossed the street and stood at the edge of the sidewalk outside the Catholic Church. The rest of the Sinful Ladies Society joined us soon after they hung up their choir robes.

We stood in a line down the sidewalk, silently waiting.

Then a peal of bells rang out and the doors to the church opened. The first person out was Celia, wearing unrelieved black and leaning on the arm of a woman I hadn't seen before.

Fifty-something, forty percent body fat, looks so much like Celia, she must be a relative.

Celia paused for just a second to look at Ida Belle, who had taken the head position in our lineup, and gave her a single nod. Then she caught sight of me and her eyes widened, then narrowed. I saw her jaw flex before she turned and continued down the sidewalk to Francine's. I caught several glares from Celia's group as they filed by.

"Maybe I shouldn't go to lunch," I said to Ida Belle. "You saw how Celia and her buddies looked at me. If it causes trouble, it only draws more attention to me."

Ida Belle shook her head. "If you don't go, you'll appear guilty."

"It looks to me like they already think I am."

"Then there's no reason to go confirming it, is there?" Ida Belle headed down the sidewalk behind the GWs, the Sinful Ladies falling in step behind her.

"She's right," Gertie said, placing her hand on my shoulder. "If you stop doing normal things, it will only add more fuel to the fire. I know it's an uncomfortable situation, but you don't have a choice. Not if we want to make the best of this."

"Fine then," I said, holding in a sigh as we started down the sidewalk after the Sinful Ladies. Ida Belle and Gertie knew this town and its residents better than anyone. If they thought this was the best course of action, I had no reason to argue. But the niggling fear that this was not going to turn out well tickled the back of my mind all the way into Francine's.

The GWs had taken the "good" tables that stretched in front of the storefront windows, the spot normally reserved for the winner of the after-church banana pudding race. Francine was already delivering bowls of banana pudding to them. I gave the bowls a wistful look as I took a seat at a table toward the back of the café.

"Runner's remorse?" Gertie whispered as we sat.

"Maybe a bit," I admitted.

"Don't worry. Next week, the pudding is ours."

"Is a week long enough to concede? I mean, with southern manners and all?"

"We're not Italian and while I won't speak ill of the dead, especially on Sunday, let's just say that everyone is mourning for Celia, not because they perceive some inherent loss to the community."

A shadow fell over my shoulder and onto the table and I looked up to see Ally holding a tray of iced tea.

"Hi, ladies," she said with a big smile, and then the next instant, she dumped the entire tray of iced tea directly on top of me.

I jumped out of my chair, startled and confused, and realized Ally was staring in shock at the woman I'd seen walk Celia out of the church. Suddenly, everything made sense. The woman must have walked up behind Ally and tipped the tray over on me.

The woman glared at me. "You've got some nerve—flaunting yourself in front of my cousin. And I saw you jogging away from her house this morning when I went to gas up the car. Haven't you caused her enough heartache? Do you have to gloat in front of her house?"

"I never set foot on your cousin's street, so you couldn't possibly have seen me there."

"I saw you jogging away from her street."

I threw my hands in the air. "She lives at the far west side of town. As long as I'm jogging east, I'll always be jogging away from her street."

"If Deputy LeBlanc had a lick of sense, you'd be sitting in jail." She narrowed her eyes. "Or maybe you're paying him off somehow. That pretty blond hair and those innocent blue eyes may fool other, less intelligent people, but I know what you are."

I struggled to maintain my cool, even though I was pretty sure I'd just been called a prostitute, or whore. I was a little confused about which. My hands clenched involuntarily and my right leg automatically slid back a couple of inches into striking position.

Ida Belle, who'd jumped up a second after me, looked at me over the woman's shoulder and shook her head. A second later, I felt a fork in my back and Gertie peered around me.

"That's enough, Dorothy," Gertie said. "You're not helping Celia any with your behavior, and we both know that when Carter has a reason to arrest anyone, he will."

"Maybe he needs some help pushing him along," Dorothy said. "Maybe I'll talk to Mayor Fontleroy about Deputy LeBlanc's job security."

"You're making a mistake," Gertie said.

"Not as big as the one you're making…taking up with murdering trash."

She spun around and stalked off toward the front section. Not even the sound of a single clinking fork could be heard in the café. Everyone sat frozen, some still holding their forks in the air. Celia looked over at me as Dorothy took a seat next to her, the faintest hint of a smile on her otherwise putrid face.

"Here's a towel," Ally said, breaking the uncomfortable silence.

She pulled a rag from her apron pocket and handed it to me.

"Show's over," Ida Belle announced. "Get back to your lunch."

Heads whipped around and everyone made a pretense of going back to their meals and previous conversations. Either people were seriously afraid of Ida Belle or they were the most conflict-avoidant group of people I'd ever seen. I leaned toward the first option.

I wiped my face with the rag, but it was like trying to drain a swimming pool with a sponge.

"Let me get you something bigger," Ally said, still looking completely horrified over the entire mess.

"No, thank you," I said. "This can't be fixed with a towel. I'm going to head home and shower. I'm sorry my presence created this mess."

Ally's face clouded in sympathy. "This is not your fault. I'll send you some lunch home with one of the Sinful Ladies."

"Thanks," I said.

"We'll go with you," Gertie said.

"No. Stay and finish your lunch."

Ida Belle frowned. "If you're alone, you don't have an alibi if anything else were to happen."

I shrugged. "Everyone I'd want to kill is in here eating lunch, so I'm good. I'll see you guys later."

I managed to hold in my frustration and embarrassment until I'd left Main Street and stepped into my neighborhood, then I kicked the first thing I saw that wouldn't break my foot. In this case, it turned out—rather appropriately—to be a wooden sign for Mayor Fontleroy's reelection campaign.

The splintering crack of the wood improved my mood, but only by a bit. With Celia's group gunning for me, I didn't stand a chance of keeping my cover intact. Once exposed, I'd have no choice but to transfer to whatever Director Morrow could muster up, and the thought of starting over in a new place depressed me.

As much as I didn't want to admit it, I kind of liked it here. Sure, I'd dug my heels straight into hell trying to keep from coming, but when you got past the drunks, idiots, and murderers, it wasn't such a bad place. In Ida Belle and Gertie I'd found comrades who understood my way of thinking and reacting as the average civilian never could. In Ally, I'd begun what could possibly turn out to be my only friendship with a civilian...and a woman to boot.

In another location, I might be safer, but I probably wouldn't matter. In Sinful, I finally felt like someone wanted me around for more reasons than earning my paycheck. I hadn't felt that way since my mother died.

"I would ticket you for destruction of private property," Deputy LeBlanc's voice sounded behind me, "but I can't stand the son of a bitch, either."

I turned around without even making an attempt at a cover story or denial. "We'd probably both be better off if you'd arrest me and lock me up."

He raised his eyebrows. "Any particular reason why?"

"Are you blind? Do you think I walk around wearing ten glasses of iced tea because I'm making a fashion statement?"

"I take it there was an accident at Francine's?"

"Oh, it was no accident. Some moose named Dorothy tipped an entire tray of tea onto me, and it's all your fault."

"How the hell is it my fault?"

"According to Dorothy, the only reason you haven't arrested me is because I'm paying you off in ways that involve no clothes and probably things that are illegal in the good town of Sinful—a fact that she announced to the entire café, I might add."

He grinned. "And that bothers you?"

"She basically called me a murderer and a whore...or prostitute. I haven't figured out which applies in this type of situation."

"Hmm, I suppose since you're receiving value for your services that would make you a prostitute."

I glared.

"Hey, at least you're a businesswoman with a purpose, although the value I'm providing seems high considering the trade."

"Excuse me? I am great at everything I do. Not that I'd ever stoop to that level, but if I did, I guarantee you, it would be well worth the cost of your deputy position in glorious Sinful, Louisiana."

He stepped closer to me and brushed a damp piece of hair from my chest, his fingers brushing lightly over the sensitive skin just above the breast-line of my dress.

"Maybe I should arrest you then. I'm probably destined for bigger things."

An unexpected flush started at my center and raced out, making every nerve ending in my body tingle. I forced myself to hold position even though the urge to take a step back was overwhelming.

"If you're going to arrest me," I said, happy that my voice sounded calm, "then I suggest you do it now, while you still have the ability."

He frowned. "What's that supposed to mean?"

"Dorothy plans on talking to the good mayor about your qualifications, or lack thereof, for doing your job, and according to the local gossip, she's not the only one riding that train. So I suggest you find the killer before they start slinging more than iced tea."

"Then I guess I better get on with it before both our good names are ruined."

I waved a hand in dismissal. "I don't have a good name to ruin."

He leaned closer to me and said in a low voice, "Then maybe you should reconsider bribing me, since you have nothing to lose."

He gave me a wink before turning around and heading off toward Main Street. I watched him walk away, unable to help admiring his perfectly proportioned backside. From broad shoulders to long, muscular legs, he was built for action. I bet he'd made a hell of a soldier.

Before my mind could wander to all the other maneuvers Deputy LeBlanc was likely highly capable of performing, I whirled around and headed home. I needed a cold shower and a new plan to stay visible without becoming an open target for

Celia and her friends.

Chapter Eleven

"We've got a problem," I said as I peeked out my living room window.

Dusk was settling over Sinful, and as soon as it turned to dark, Ida Belle, Gertie, and I were going to break into the sheriff's department and find out what was in Pansy's file.

Ida Belle stepped up behind me. "What's wrong?"

I lifted a slat on the blinds and pointed to the ancient horse with even older rider standing across the street. "Surveillance."

Ida Belle peered outside. "Oh, for heaven's sake."

She turned and yelled down the hall to Gertie, who was in the kitchen, changing into tennis shoes.

"Carter's got Sheriff Lee sitting across the street."

Gertie hurried up front, pulling on a black crocheted sweater as she came.

"I said black hoodie," Ida Belle said. "We're going to a break-in, not a funeral."

"This is the best I could do on short notice," Gertie said. "I have a black hat to match."

Ida Belle rolled her eyes. "Lovely. If we get caught, you'll have the most fashionable mug shot. Fortune managed to come up with a black hoodie."

"Ladies," I interrupted, not bothering to point out that out of habit, I'd bought every black hoodie in my size at the General Store. "We have bigger issues, remember?"

Gertie stepped over to the window and took a look. "No problem. Give me a minute."

I looked over at Ida Belle, who shrugged as Gertie hustled back to the kitchen. A minute later, I heard the microwave sound off, then seconds later, Gertie came back down the hall carrying a small plate of cookies and a glass of milk.

"Can someone get the door?" she asked.

I opened the door for her and she walked across the street to talk with Sheriff Lee.

"Is she really trying to bribe him with milk and cookies?" I asked.

"Heck if I know," Ida Belle said.

I watched as Gertie motioned to Sheriff Lee to dismount. After several shaky minutes, he managed to arrive upright on my neighbor's lawn. He took another excruciating couple of minutes to tie the horse to a tree, then even longer to lower himself down to a sitting position with his back against the tree.

Gertie handed him the milk and cookies, and he gave her a huge smile. She trotted back to my house, waving over her shoulder as she went. Once inside, she slumped against the living room wall, trying to catch her breath.

Before Ida Belle could say a word, Gertie held up her hand.

"I know," she wheezed. "I've got to get in better shape."

I shook my head. "How in the world did you guys ever win the banana pudding race with Gertie as your representative?" The rest of the Sinful Ladies sang in choir and weren't available for the dash. Gertie was tone-deaf, so the availability was there but the capability was seriously lacking.

"Before you came," Ida Belle explained, "someone would take off from choir duty that day—usually me. I'm thinking of having mandatory PT twice a week. The crew is getting soft."

I didn't bother to point out that most of the crew was well beyond the backside of peak performance. But considering the competition wasn't in any better shape, I supposed it was all relative.

"I don't get it," I said, returning to the business at hand. "What does giving him milk and cookies accomplish?"

"Give it a minute to work," Gertie said and motioned to the window.

We peered out across the street as the setting sun disappeared over the next row of houses. The streetlights flickered on, illuminating the sheriff as he chugged the last bit of milk and put the glass on the ground next to him on top of the plate.

"Watch closely," Gertie said. "One, two three…"

Before she reached four, Sheriff Lee's head bobbed once, then fell to his chest as his whole body slumped. The horse, following his rider's lead, leaned against the tree and closed his eyes.

A burst of panic shot through me as for an instant, I thought she'd killed him, then I remembered I was in Sinful, not Iraq, and realigned my thinking.

"Did you slip some cough medicine in the milk?"

"Of course not! That would be wasteful."

"You're telling me that milk and cookies knocked him out?"

"*Warm* milk and cookies. I bring him a plate of cookies every time I make a new batch. His wife's been gone for a long while and he really misses her homemade cookies. After two or three, he nods off and I let myself out. He went even faster tonight."

"Makes sense," Ida Belle said. "It's a couple hours past his bedtime."

Technically, Sheriff Lee was several decades beyond life expectancy, much less bedtime, but I figured it would be rude to point it out. "How long will he sleep?"

Gertie shrugged. "Until morning, unless it rains or someone wakes him up."

"Well, let's get out of here before it rains or the neighbor notices his oak tree is holding up a man and a horse."

Ida Belle had docked her boat in the bayou behind my house, so we headed out the back door and hopped in the small flat-bottom boat. The bayou ran behind the east side of Main Street, allowing us to dock right behind the sheriff's department, cutting down our risk of being seen.

After taking her seat on the middle bench, Gertie pulled on her black crocheted hat. Ida Belle gave the flowered pattern one glance and shook her head. I held in a smile as she started the boat and set off down the bayou toward town.

The sheriff's boat was docked at the pier directly

behind the building, the floodlight from the back of the building casting a dim glow over the dock. Ida Belle eased her boat up beside the sheriff's boat where it couldn't be seen, and we climbed over the sheriff's boat to the dock.

"I know we have the security code, but how are we supposed to get in?" I asked. "Did Myrtle give you a key?"

Ida Belle shook her head. "She only has a key to the front door, and Carter checks the back door before leaving every night, so it wouldn't do any good for her to leave it unlocked."

I looked at the thick set of hedges that ran across the back side of the building. "Please tell me we don't have to go in through a window."

"We don't have to go in through a window," Ida Belle said. "*You* have to lift me up to the window and I'll let you and Gertie in the back door."

Suddenly, Ida Belle's insistence that they couldn't do this without me made sense. "I suppose it would have been too much of a stretch to just bring a ladder?"

"If something goes wrong, a ladder would give us away. Not like we could run with one."

I probably could, but I saw her point. If a quick getaway were necessary, leaving the ladder behind would give Carter a clear idea what was going on, and taking it with us presented some logistics problems in the boat.

"Fine, then let's get on with it before Father Time wakes up and alerts Carter that we're gone."

Gertie went to the back door and pulled out the piece of paper with the alarm code. I put my hands in front of my face and pushed through the hedge to the back side, glad I'd worn long sleeves and gloves. The sharp branches of the hedge would have shredded my skin.

Ida Belle stepped beside me and gave Gertie a thumbs-up. Gertie punched in the code and we heard a single beep inside. I leaned over and linked my hands together, creating a stirrup for Ida Belle to step in.

As soon as she stepped in my hands, I pulled my arms up and tossed her up the side of the building, praying that she had great balance. As soon as her foot left my hands, I spun around and caught her feet as she grabbed hold of the window sill, then held her in place while she lifted the window. One last push by me and she was over the ledge and in the building.

I heard a loud thump and something breaking on the floor inside. I cringed and hoped it wasn't Ida Belle that had broken. She peered over the ledge a couple of seconds later and gave me a wave. I pushed back through the hedge, then joined Gertie at the back door, instantly shifting into high alert as if I were on a CIA mission.

Something rattled next to the steps and I automatically reached for the nine millimeter that wasn't there. Gertie sucked in a breath and we leaned over the steps in time to see a furry face peek out of the trash can.

"It's just a raccoon," Gertie whispered.

I'd had a run-in with a raccoon in my attic as soon as I arrived in Sinful. As "know your enemy" was a religion for CIA agents, research was in order. I'd been surprised to find they were kind of cute, in a loud, nuisance sort of way, but their dexterity was even more impressive and exhibited clearly why God hadn't given opposable thumbs to some of the larger, man-eating creatures.

Feeling as if we'd been standing there forever, I glanced down at my watch, but only a minute had elapsed since I'd pitched Ida Belle up at the window. I heard the door jiggle, and Ida Belle swung open the door and motioned us inside.

We'd already decided that flashlights were too risky, so we all had glow sticks instead. The soft green light wasn't bright, but it would provide enough illumination to navigate the office without running into things.

"What did you break?" I asked, hoping it wasn't something noticeable or expensive.

"Just a tea glass," Ida Belle said. "I'll pick up the pieces to bring with us when we leave."

I nodded. "I guess the file will be in Carter's office?"

"That's my guess," Ida Belle said. "It's this way."

Gertie and I followed Ida Belle down a short hallway and into an office.

"Spread out and look for the file," I said. "I'll jimmy the file cabinet."

I pulled out a knife and went to work on the metal cabinet while Ida Belle and Gertie dug through the desk and credenza. Opening the cabinet was an easy task for someone with my skill set and only seconds later, I was flipping through files.

It didn't take long to realize that what we were looking for wasn't there. "Any luck?" I asked as I pushed the cabinet drawers shut and locked it again.

"Nothing," Gertie said.

"Me, either," Ida Belle said.

I reached for the trash can and pulled out an envelope. "It's from the coroner in New Orleans—delivered by courier."

"Then where is the report?" Gertie asked.

Ida Belle shook her head. "I think we've underestimated Carter."

"He took it home with him," I said.

Ida Belle nodded. "It certainly looks that way."

A sliver of fear ran through me. Clearly, Carter expected someone—likely us—to attempt to get information on the case. He'd changed his computer password, required all information be delivered by courier, and had taken the file with him when he left the office.

"Why didn't he change the security code?" I asked.

Ida Belle frowned. "I don't know."

"It doesn't make sense," I said, "given the other lengths he's gone to."

Ida Belle paled. "He set us up. I bet the security company was on the phone with him ten seconds after we entered the building."

Gertie's eyes widened. "We have to get out."

I dropped the envelope back in the trash can and turned the office chair the same direction it had been when we entered the room. "Don't panic. Ida Belle, run upstairs, collect that broken glass, and climb out the window. I'll be ready for you. Gertie will start the boat."

We'd barely made it out Carter's office door when I heard his monster truck pulling up in front of the building.

"Run!" Gertie yelled and bolted for the back

door.

For the first time since I'd met her, Ida Belle looked panicked.

"The glass—the window?"

"Forget it," I said and pulled her arm as I took off down the hallway behind Gertie. "He can't prove anything if he can't catch us."

I heard Ida Belle's steps pounding behind me and she was only seconds behind as I shot out the door. Gertie was already halfway to the bayou. I could hear keys rattling in the front door.

"We'll never make it to the boat," Ida Belle whispered.

Years of training took over and I vaulted over the railing to the ground. I grabbed the trash can and ran back up the steps, ignoring Ida Belle, who was staring at me like I'd lost my mind. I lay the trash can flat in the door opening and pulled the lid off.

The raccoon shot out of the trash can and into the office. As I pulled the door shut, Ida Belle sprang into action, hauling the trash can back to its spot. I jumped up on the tiny metal railing, loosened the bulb in the security light until it blinked out, leaving only the dim light from neighboring buildings to light the lawn. Then I jumped off the railing and ran for the bayou.

I heard a giant crash inside the office and then Carter cursing, but I didn't take the time to glance back. Gertie had the boat pulled up to the bank and I vaulted into it right behind Ida Belle, who had surprised me with both her speed and her dexterity.

As soon as my feet hit the bottom of the boat, Gertie launched the boat in reverse, throwing me down in the bottom. I peered over the edge of the boat as Gertie changed gears and slammed straight into the big wave she'd created backing up, sending a sheet of water over the boat. I ducked just in time to keep my eyeballs from getting drenched, but the rest of me was not as lucky.

Ida Belle pulled a towel out of the bench she was sitting on and tossed it to me before plopping back down and holding on for her life. Apparently, my drenching was of no concern to Gertie, who never reduced her speed the slightest bit, instead barreling down the bayou at full speed, weaving like a drunk. I refused to even think about the fact that she wasn't wearing her glasses.

The back door to the sheriff's department flew open and light from inside the office illuminated the exit. The raccoon raced outside and made a beeline for the trees. Carter paused long enough to close the door, then ran for the dock.

My pulse rate ticked into overdrive.

"He's going to catch us," I said. Ida Belle's tiny outboard motor was no match for the monster power on the sheriff's boat.

"We'll beat him to your house," Ida Belle said, but her expression was grim.

"But we won't make it inside," I said. "And I'm soaked."

"We don't have to make it inside," Ida Belle said. "I have a backup plan."

I closed my eyes and said a prayer, not sure whether to be relieved or scared.

"Take off your sweatshirt," Ida Belle said.

I looked up and realized that she had already shrugged off her sweatshirt and shoved it into a trash bag along with hers and Gertie's gloves. I pulled off the sweatshirt and gloves and tossed them both in the bag. Ida Belle dropped a small anchor in the trash bag, tied it closed and flung it into the middle of the bayou, where it immediately dropped out of sight.

"Right!" Ida Belle yelled at Gertie.

I swung around just in time to see the bank approaching my face at a rapid pace. I clutched the side of the boat as Gertie cut the motor hard and held my breath as the boat slammed into the bank, then continued in the right direction. The turn took us out of town and into the suburb. I studied the houses as we flew past, trying to estimate how far we were from mine. I could hear the roar of the sheriff's boat echoing behind us and knew he was closing in fast.

"Left!" Ida Belle shouted.

All of a sudden, Gertie swung the boat to the left and headed straight for land. I could see the bank rapidly approaching, but Gertie showed no sign of slowing.

"Cut the engine!" Ida Belle yelled, but it was too little, too late.

Chapter Twelve

The momentum vaulted the boat straight up the sloping bank and into the row of azalea bushes, bouncing Gertie clean out of the boat. Then it slammed into the trunk of a particularly large bush and launched me forward out of the boat and onto the lawn. Instantly, I tucked and rolled, then yanked a branch from my pants as I vaulted up and ran after Ida Belle, who'd fled the boat and was now dragging Gertie toward the bank.

"Hurry up!" she yelled back at me.

I had no idea why she was running for the bayou and not the house when Deputy LeBlanc was going to pull up any second. Even more disconcerting was the fact that I took off behind them like it made good sense.

When I reached the bank, Ida Belle cast a fishing pole and shoved it at me. I took the pole and watched as she cast another. I glanced over and realized Gertie was sitting in one of three lawn chairs stretched across the bank, none of which belonged to me or had been on my lawn earlier that afternoon.

At the roar of a boat engine, I yanked my head

around and saw the lights from the sheriff's boat round the corner toward my house.

"Sit down," Ida Belle ordered. "You're calling attention to yourself."

I plopped into the middle chair, convinced this was the worst backup plan ever. No way was he going to believe we were fishing.

A couple of seconds later, the sheriff's boat coasted to the bank about twenty feet from us. The floodlights on top of his boat illuminated a huge stretch of the bank, including where we sat. One look at his face was all it took to know he was hopping mad.

He jumped onto the bank and immediately zeroed in on Ida Belle's boat, which rested halfway in the azalea hedge. Shaking his head, he strode toward us. "What do you think you're doing?"

Ida Belle looked up at him and her confused expression was so good she almost had me fooled. "Fishing," she said. Her eyes widened and she looked up at the moon. "It's not a waning gibbous, is it?"

Gertie leaned forward in her chair and I realized that not only was she still wearing her black crocheted hat but a couple of small branches were stuck in the yarn and standing up on top of her head.

"It's illegal to fish on Sundays when it's a waning gibbous," Gertie said to me.

Of course it is.

"Hey, isn't it against the rules to work on Sundays?" I asked. "Should we be fishing?"

Gertie waved a hand in dismissal. "Fishing isn't work. And that whole not working on Sundays thing is Biblical, not Sinful, law, so we'd only be in danger from God, not Carter." She looked up at him and gave him a broad smile.

The look on Deputy LeBlanc's face left me no doubt who we should be most afraid of.

"Don't even try to convince me you've been here all evening," he said.

"Of course not." Ida Belle looked indignant. "We had supper first. If something's bothering you, Carter, I wish you'd just spit it out."

He narrowed his eyes at us. "I just came from the sheriff's department. A window was open upstairs and a raccoon wreaked havoc on the place before I got him back outside."

"Those things are sneaky," I said. "I never would have believed it if I hadn't seen that one open the window in my attic. Damned amazing, if you ask me."

"I didn't ask you," Carter said, "and I'm far from amazed because I'm quite certain the raccoon did not unlock the back door, nor did he attempt to disarm the alarm using an outdated code."

"Why didn't he use the new code?" Gertie asked.

"Damn it!" Carter yelled. "I know you three broke into that building. I ought to do Sinful a favor and lock you all up and throw away the key."

"Take that tone with me again," Ida Belle said, her voice dripping with disapproval, "and I'll speak to your mother. Now, I've already said we ate supper, then came out here to fish."

"Uh-huh," Carter said, "then where's the fish?"

Ida Belle reached over and lifted the top on an ice chest that stood next to her chair. I leaned over and barely controlled my surprise at the three fish flopping around inside. I officially revised my opinion of Ida Belle and her backup plan. She was good!

Carter looked down at the fish, then over at me. "Why is she wet?"

An image of a failed fishing trip with my father flashed through my mind as if it were yesterday. "Ida Belle was trying to teach me to cast," I said, "but I threw the whole rod out into the bayou, so I had to wade in and get it."

He stared at me, eye to eye, as I delivered my story, but Deputy LeBlanc had definitely met his match. I'd lied successfully and without qualm to some of the most dangerous men in the world. The deputy was smart, but compared to the men I'd fooled, he was an amateur.

Apparently, Deputy LeBlanc figured out he would get nowhere with me as well, so he turned his attention to Gertie, the perceived weak link in the chain. I felt my stomach clench just a bit as he studied her. I still hadn't determined how much of Gertie's fluffy, confused, old-lady demeanor was real versus act.

Gertie appeared oblivious to his scrutiny, slowly reeling in her line as if she were truly concentrating on fishing. Deputy LeBlanc stepped closer to her and narrowed his eyes.

"I suppose you're sticking with the fishing story as well?" he asked.

She looked up at him and the look of confusion on her face was Academy Award–winning. "Why do you think we're lying when you see us fishing? You've even seen the fish."

"Do you always fish with a hat on?"

"My ears get cold."

"It's ninety degrees outside."

"When you're old, your blood thins."

"Uh-huh." He pulled a branch from her hat and held it in front of her face. "And this is what…camouflage? Are you afraid the fish will see your cap and stop biting?"

She grabbed the branch from his hand and shoved it back in her hat. "Azalea leaves keep the mosquitoes away."

"I've lived here almost thirty years and never heard that, but I find it most interesting that the night you choose to wear the hedges is the same night I find Ida Belle's boat docked halfway up the lawn in the middle of them."

Gertie waved her hand in dismissal. "We just hid it there to keep boat thieves from taking it."

Deputy LeBlanc's eyes widened. "There are no boat thieves in Sinful."

"A boat got stolen from the Swamp Bar last week," Gertie said.

Deputy LeBlanc closed his eyes and shook his head. "You're hardly at risk of being the *victim* of theft when you're the *perpetrator*."

I fought the overwhelming urge to laugh, as he'd gotten that exactly right. I managed to cover it with a cough, but just as I lifted my hand to cover my mouth, something tugged on my fishing line—hard. I'd seen the line before Ida Belle cast it and it had been sans bait, so the fact that something had been foolish enough to bite an empty hook had me wondering if maybe the water in Sinful was what prevented everyone from being normal.

"There's something on my line," I said.

"Goody, goody!" Gertie jumped up and clapped

her hands.

For a split second, Ida Belle looked just as confused as I felt, but she quickly recovered and jumped up to instruct me.

"Grip the pole here and here," she said and pushed my hands into the correct position. "Then pull the pole back to draw in the fish, lower the pole, and reel in the slack. Keep doing that until you get the fish out of the water. And for Christ's sake, Carter, move out of the way!"

Carter moved to the side, looked completely aggrieved, but without saying a word. As soon as I had a clear view, I pulled back on the pole, then started reeling, then I pulled and reeled again, then again.

Good God, fishing was a bore.

Hoping to end this yawn-fest sometime this century, I yanked the pole back as far as I could. Unfortunately, I didn't have much line left to reel.

The end of the line popped out of the bayou, fish attached, and came flying at the bank. Carter, who'd been looking back at me, picked that moment to turn around and got hit across the face with the flying fish.

Horrified, I stood there frozen, no earthly idea what kind of apology this situation required. Ida Belle started laughing and dropped into her lawn chair so hard, it flipped straight over backward, pitching her onto the lawn but not hard enough to stop her laughter. Gertie immediately set to trying to capture the flopping fish that seemed to leap out of her grasp every time she wrapped her hands around it.

Carter wiped his cheek with his hand, looking

mad enough to spit. "Bottom line," he said. "I may not have proof that you stole that boat last week at the Swamp Bar, and I may not have proof that you broke into the sheriff's department tonight, but I know what I know."

He pointed his finger and stared at each one of us for several uncomfortable seconds. "I'm only going to say this one time—stay out of my investigation!"

He whirled around to leave, but before he made it two steps, a man's voice sounded behind us.

"Deputy LeBlanc?" the man called as he hurried across my back lawn. "I thought I heard your voice."

Despite the fact that he wasn't wearing his usual uptight suit and tie, I recognized the man as my neighbor from across the street.

"Yes, Mr. Foster," Deputy LeBlanc said. "What can I do for you?"

Mr. Foster stopped in front of us and put his hands on his hips, causing his sweatpants to rise to mid-calf, exposing legs that looked like a chicken's. "I have a pile of horse crap in my front lawn the size of a grown man. What does the sheriff's department intend to do about it?"

Unable to help myself, I perked up. "Isn't it illegal for horses to crap on lawns on Sundays?"

"No," Gertie said, standing there clutching the fish in her hat and wearing a grin like a serial killer. "It's only illegal if they do it in the street. It's just rude if they do it in the lawn."

Ida Belle nodded. "Especially if it's someone else's lawn."

Deputy LeBlanc glared at us, then swung around and stalked toward the street, Mr. Foster in tow.

Gertie succeeded in removing the fish from the hook and tossed it in the ice chest with the others before taking her seat. Ida Belle picked herself up from the lawn, righted her chair, and sat back down, her cheeks wet from her hysterical laughing-crying jag. I would have preferred to go straight inside into the shower, and then down a shot of Sinful Ladies cough syrup, put on my noise-canceling headphones and climb into bed, but it was only ten o'clock and chicken that I was, I didn't want Deputy LeBlanc to catch me alone if he decided to pay another visit that night.

So I plopped back down into my chair with a sigh. When was I going to learn not to get involved with Gertie and Ida Belle's "foolproof" plans?

"You want me to cast your line?" Ida Belle asked.

"No! There wasn't even bait on that hook. The fish here are as crazy as the residents."

"Probably true," Gertie agreed.

"You know," Ida Belle said, giving me a sideways look. "We're going to have to work on your pickup technique."

"What? I…"

Gertie nodded. "She's right. Slapping a man across the face with a fish hasn't been sexy since the fifties."

Ida Belle started to chuckle again. "Maybe she's a traditionalist."

Gertie smiled. "Or maybe she's older than she looks."

"I *am* older than I look. Knowing you two has aged me at least fifty years."

I slumped down in the chair and closed my eyes,

giving them their thirty seconds of laughter at my expense…again, then I sat up and looked at them.

"We are running out of options for information," I said.

Instantly, they shifted from jovial to serious.

"I've been thinking," Ida Belle said. "Do you remember the name of the coroner on that envelope?"

"Yeah," I said, then a bolt of fear ran through me. "No way! We are not breaking into the coroner's office. The New Orleans police will *not* be as lenient as Carter has been."

"I don't think we have to break in," Ida Belle said and pulled her cell phone from her pocket.

"You know someone in the coroner's office?" I asked, praying that it could be something that simple.

"No," Ida Belle said, "but I know someone who does some side work for the funeral home. They'll probably prepare the body in New Orleans before they ship it back to Sinful for burial."

"She means Genesis," Gertie said as Ida Belle rose from her chair and walked off, talking on her phone.

"Hairstylist Genesis?"

Gertie nodded. "Remember we told you she does makeup in the arts district for plays and such. Well, the director of the funeral home that most people in Sinful use saw one of the plays and asked about the makeup artist. He pays her a fortune to do makeup on the more difficult cases."

I shook my head. I was as hard as they came, but the thought of applying makeup to corpses made me grimace just a little. "But we don't know what

Pansy's body looks like. She may not be a difficult case."

"No," Ida Belle said, "but with Genesis being from Sinful and knowing Pansy, she might be able to convince the funeral director to let her do the makeup as a special favor to Celia. Give me a minute."

She pulled out her cell phone and walked several feet away.

"Hey," I said and looked over at Gertie. "What are we going to do with those fish, anyway?"

Gertie gave the ice chest a wistful glance, then sighed. "Those are some really nice trout, but I suppose we should put them back in Walter's stock tank."

"You stole the fish from Walter?"

"No. We *borrowed* the fish from Walter. Besides, we're bringing back an extra. That seems fair."

I opened my mouth to reply, but couldn't come up with anything.

Ida Belle slipped her phone back in her pocket and walked back over to our chairs. "She's going to call the funeral director first thing tomorrow."

"Are you sure we should involve more people in this? Ally is already sticking her neck out trying to get in Pansy's closet tomorrow. I don't want anyone getting into trouble on my account."

"Genesis is happy to do it," Ida Belle said. "Hell, if she still lived in Sinful, she'd be as big a suspect as you. Those two have a seriously checkered past."

"Let me guess," I said. "Pansy slept with Genesis' boyfriend?"

"Boyfriends," Gertie said. "Plural."

I threw my hands in the air. "Are there any men under the age of forty that Pansy *didn't* sleep with?"

Gertie's brow wrinkled in concentration. "There was…no, prom night…what about…never mind, I forgot about that fiasco at the funeral. No, not that I know of."

"I can't think of anyone," Ida Belle said then frowned. "Except maybe Carter."

Gertie's eyes widened. "You're right. Pansy starting chasing him in the crib, but he always steered clear of her. Some of us thought he went into the service to get away from Pansy as much as to get away from Sinful."

I frowned. "Doesn't that seem odd to you? I mean, I barely knew the woman and I'm certain I didn't like her, but she had that look that most men go for—at least for one night."

Ida Belle nodded. "Men *do* love a skank."

Gertie gave her a disapproving look. "You really shouldn't talk that way considering she's dead. It's not polite."

Ida Belle waved a hand in dismissal. "I stopped being polite back in the fifties, and I'm not interested in rewriting history, especially when Fortune is on the hook for this unless we can figure out which of the many people who hated Pansy finally had the nerve to kill her."

"Politeness is overrated and in high supply here," I said. "What we don't have enough of is the truth."

"Preach," Ida Belle said.

"So back to my original question," I continued. "Why would a teenage Carter avoid a sure thing?"

"He had a girlfriend," Gertie said.

"He did not," Ida Belle argued. "I think I'd

remember if he did. My mind is in excellent shape."

"She didn't live here," Gertie said. "Remember, when he was in high school, he made those trips into New Orleans every weekends."

"He was working construction," Ida Belle said. "He always came back with money."

Gertie nodded. "Yes, but construction jobs don't require you to show up with a newly washed truck. He had that old truck of his in the driveway every Friday afternoon, hosing it down and polishing it until it shined."

Ida Belle frowned. "You may be right. I wonder what happened?"

"Young love ends for hundreds of different reasons," Gertie said and sighed.

Ida Belle nodded. "But usually, life strangles it to death."

I slumped back down in my chair and stared out over the bayou, Ida Belle's comment making me wonder. Had she loved someone years ago? Perhaps someone in Sinful who wanted the traditional wife that Ida Belle was never going to be? Or maybe a soldier who didn't make it out of Vietnam, or returned to his own life back home?

And as much as I hated to admit it, I wondered about Carter and his secret love. Had she broken his heart? Had he enlisted to escape the painful memories of what could have been?

It was all so hard for me to understand. I'd never been in love—wasn't even sure I knew what it felt like. I'd loved my mother and she died. I'd loved my father, but he didn't love me. Had I written off love in my childhood? Had I let my father's failings cloud my future?

I picked up the fishing pole and cast the line in the bayou.

I had plenty of questions, but I wasn't ready for some of the answers.

Chapter Thirteen

I'd already been up and pacing for two hours before my cell phone rang. I checked the display—the General Store. Ida Belle or Gertie must have given Walter my number.

"Good morning, Sunshine," Walter said when I answered.

I smiled. I really liked Walter, and it was hard not to smile when a man you liked called you Sunshine. "Good morning, Walter. What can I do for you?"

"It's not what you can do for me, but what I can do for you. Guess what came in first thing this morning on my delivery truck?"

"The battery for the Jeep?"

"You got it. If you aren't busy, I can send Scooter to tow the Jeep in and get that battery installed this morning. Since the Jeep hasn't moved in a while, I'd like to do an oil change and have Scooter give it a once-over. He's available now if you're ready."

"Absolutely."

I was already dressed in shorts and a tank top, so I tossed the phone on the kitchen counter and reached for my tennis shoes, still smiling with excitement. Part of Marge's estate included an older model Jeep—one of those from back when Jeeps were rugged, manly vehicles and not hip commuters for urban yuppies. Because it had sat so long, the battery was dead, but Walter had ordered one as soon as I arrived in Sinful. I couldn't wait to get my own set of wheels. Between Ida Belle's five million rules surrounding her Corvette and Gertie's refusal to wear glasses, transportation had been a sketchy proposition.

I watched out the front window as the tow truck circled the block three times. As giant iron house numbers hung above the garage door and the door was already open, displaying the Jeep needing a tow, it was a little disconcerting. But I was willing to give him a pass for sunlight glare or perhaps dyslexia. Finally, on the fourth trip around, I walked out the front door and waved my arms to get his attention. He slammed on the brakes, then backed the tow truck in the driveway before getting out to greet me.

Five foot ten. A hundred forty pounds—maybe. Early twenties. Decent muscle tone in the arms. Legs like a chicken. Threat level one...if he were driving the truck.

My assessment put Scooter somewhere just about the twenty-year mark, but he looked fifteen and acted twelve. His jaw dropped so much when I introduced myself that I was afraid a small bird might nest in it. Apparently, he hadn't gotten the memo on required manners in Sinful, because he spent the entire time we shook hands staring at my chest. When he started to shake harder, I figured it was time to cease with the pleasantries.

"You need any help?" I asked, thinking it was a loaded question as soon as it left my mouth.

He peered inside at the Jeep. "Nope. Since you backed it in the garage, it will be easy to tow."

He returned to his truck to position it in front of the Jeep. I didn't bother explaining that if the Jeep had been drivable enough for me to back it in, I wouldn't need a tow. He didn't seem capable of processing a lot of information at once, and as he would have my only shot at private transportation hanging by a hook, I figured it was best to let him direct all two brain cells to that activity alone.

I watched as he made quick work of lifting the Jeep, somewhat surprised at his speed and dexterity. Apparently, all of Scooter's skill set was concentrated around motor vehicles.

"If you aren't busy, ma'am," Scooter said when he'd gotten the Jeep in position, "Walter would like to see you. He said to tell you he has fresh-baked coffee cake."

He had me at "Walter would like to see you," but the coffee cake definitely sweetened the deal. Aside from this morning, Walter had never contacted me, and certainly hadn't asked for a meeting. My curiosity was definitely piqued.

"I can give you a lift to the store," Scooter said, looking entirely too hopeful.

What the hell. The guy probably didn't get a lot of thrills in Sinful. If staring at my cleavage for a couple of blocks made his day, it was my good deed for the day. Besides, it wasn't like the rest of Sinful was clamoring to see me, so even the adoration of this clearly juvenile male was a bit of an ego boost.

"Sure. Give me a minute to lock up."

Scooter was still grinning from ear to ear when I returned from retrieving my purse and locking up. He fell all over himself rushing in front of me to open the passenger door of the tow truck. I knew he was going to look at my rear when I climbed up into the cab, but short of climbing up backward, I didn't see that it was avoidable.

He was still standing there, grinning and starstruck, when I finished buckling my seat belt. I waved a hand in front of his face. "Coffee cake is waiting. Let's move."

"Yes, ma'am," he said and raced around the truck, then scrambled inside.

For a moment, I was worried he'd tear out of the driveway and drag-race to the General Store, but he eased across the dip where the driveway met the street, then started toward Main Street at a moderate speed. He stopped in front of the store to let me out, then headed for the corner where the service bay was located. I noticed he waited until I was all the way inside the store before turning.

Walter was at his usual seat behind the counter and waved as I walked inside. He gave me a broad smile and gestured to a stool on the other side of the counter.

"Perfect timing," he said and pointed to the coffeepot at the end of the counter next to the cash register. "It just finished brewing."

"Then what are you waiting for?" I asked as I slid onto the stool. "Break out the cake."

He went into the back room and came back with two huge slices of coffee cake. Unable to wait any longer, I took a bite of the cake while he poured the coffee. The perfect blend of light cake with a hint of cinnamon had me sighing with pleasure.

Walter slid my coffee across the counter. "I take it you like it?"

"This is quite possibly the best thing I've ever eaten, and that's saying a lot given the food I've consumed since I've been in Sinful."

He smiled. "You're so much easier to please than the other women in this town."

"Don't let word of my weakness get back to Scooter. I have a feeling he'd be standing on my doorstep every day with a coffee cake."

Walter laughed. "Scooter may be a little dim on some things but he's hell with engines, and in this case, I'd have to agree with his taste in women. He's a nice guy. You could do a lot worse…especially in Sinful."

I took a sip of coffee and shook my head. "No matter how nice, I'm not interested."

"Why? You have a problem dating nice guys?"

"I do if I can beat them up—general rule."

"Well, I guess that leaves me out."

"For you, I'd make an exception."

"Ha. I've been chasing a woman like you for over forty years. All it's gotten me is callouses."

I studied him for a minute. He wasn't Sean Connery, but Walter was a nice-looking man. I think it had something to do with his smile and his easy manner with people. So he was nice-looking, had a dry sense of humor that I immensely appreciated, and owned one of the mainstay businesses in town. For the life of me, I couldn't figure out why Ida Belle kept turning him down. Surely, giving up the helm of the Sinful Ladies

Society wasn't enough to keep her from having a relationship with an attractive, available man. Was it?

"I don't get it," I said, deciding I couldn't keep my opinion to myself. "Why do you keep chasing her if she's not interested?"

"Who said she wasn't interested?" He grinned. "She's interested all right. Ida Belle's just stubborn is all."

"Well, not to offend either of you, but I hope she loosens up before you both die."

Walter choked on his coffee, wheezing and laughing at the same time. "You are quite the breath of fresh air in a town of hidden agendas and hypocritical politeness."

"Is that why you invited me for coffee cake?"

He sobered and shook his head. "I'm afraid my reasons for that weren't near as pleasant as discussing our potential for dating in this town."

I felt my heart drop. If Walter had plied me with sweets as an opener, what he had to say couldn't possibly be good.

"Lay it on me," I said, hoping to ease the discomfort he clearly felt. "Nothing you say could surprise me at this point."

He nodded. "I suppose that's true." He took a deep breath and leaned across the counter, even though we were the only people in the store.

"Friday night about ten, me and Shorty, the butcher, were standing around the side street at the mechanic's bay, watching a couple of bull gators that were scrapping in the bayou behind the shops. I heard heels click across the wooden entry mat that Shorty has in front of his shop, then I heard Pansy talking."

"Who was she talking to?" I asked.

He shook his head. "Wasn't no one else there, so I guess she was talking to herself. Pansy always did like the sound of her own voice."

"I assume she was talking about me?"

"She didn't name any names, but she was ranting. Said, 'That bitch isn't going to ruin this for me. By the time I'm done, her and her fake blond hair will be crawling back under whatever rock she came out from under.'"

Okay. It wasn't the nicest thing someone could say about me, but it wasn't exactly damning. "Is that it?"

"No. I heard her dialing, then the next thing she said was, 'Meet me at my house tonight at midnight. We have a business matter to discuss.' Then the heels went clicking away."

I perked up. "That's great news! All they have to do is check Pansy's cell phone and see who she called. That lets me out of it."

"I'm afraid it's not that easy," Walter said. "I overheard Carter talking to the forensics team. They're looking for Pansy's cell phone, but I don't think they've found it."

Shit! As Ida Belle would say—this was not good. I looked across the counter at Walter, who looked absolutely miserable. "Please don't feel bad about this, Walter. You didn't have any choice but to tell Carter. This is a murder investigation and he's your nephew."

Walter straightened up and frowned. "Oh, hell, I didn't tell Carter anything and won't. I think I'm smart enough to know a murderer when I see one, and you don't fit the bill."

"Thank you," I said and smiled. If he only knew.

"But that idiot Shorty is feeling guilty and I think he's going to cave. He tried to convince me to say something, but I played dumb and told him I didn't hear anything as my right ear's been clogged. He wants to be a snitch, that's all on him."

"I imagine most people don't like being involved in something like this."

"Talking to the police is what will involve him. Keeping his mouth shut doesn't hurt anyone."

I frowned, thinking about the conversation that Walter had overheard. "I don't get it. I mean, the first part of it, clearly she's bitching about me. But then she shifted gears and made the phone call. So who did she want to meet at midnight for a business discussion? And what kind of business?"

"I been racking my brain on that one for days. I just don't know."

"But we have to assume that it was the murderer."

Walter nodded. "Seems to be the case."

"Pansy has been gone from Sinful for years. What kind of business would she have with someone here?"

"Blackmail was the first thing that came to my mind, but then I've never thought all that highly of the girl or her mother."

Considering what I knew about Pansy's little IRS problem, blackmail sounded like a really good bet. "Any ideas who she had on the hook?"

He shook his head. "It could be anybody male. Most every man in Sinful's been looking over his shoulder and holding onto his wife a little tighter since Pansy got back into town. She probably had the juice to cause problems with any number of them."

"Do any of them have the money to pay?"

"I'd say several of them do. Not LA kind of money, but some of the guys Pansy ran with in high school work construction in New Orleans. Others work on oil rigs. They make enough to afford nice houses, pickup trucks, and bass boats, and none of their wives work."

"So she might not get rich off of any one of them, but if she hit up all of them, she might be able to leave Sinful with quite a nest egg."

Walter nodded. "You got it."

I blew out a breath. "But how do I prove it?"

"*That* is the sixty-four-thousand-dollar question."

The bells above the front door jangled. Walter glanced at the front of the store, then frowned. "It's the mayor's wife," he said, his voice low.

It took every ounce of self-control for me not to whip my head around and get a look at the woman who had been worth half of the mayor's money. I was willing to bet anything that she wasn't worth it.

I heard heels clicking on the hardwood floor and finally, they came to a stop beside me. I looked up into the disapproving stare of an attempted-and-failed Marilyn Monroe look-alike.

A very worn mid-forties. A hundred forty pounds, but she probably lies and says one hundred ten. Fake hair, nails, eye color, nose, boobs, and God only knows what else.

What the hell was the mayor thinking?

"How unfortunate," she said and wrinkled her

nose. "I don't shop with trash, so if you'll just be on your way, then I can handle my business."

I didn't bother moving from my stool. I was afraid if I stood up, I'd hit her. "You've got some nerve swinging that trash label around, Wife Number Two."

Her face flushed red and she glared. "I asked you politely to leave. Now, I'm telling you. Get out of here or I'll call the police."

"That's enough, Vanessa," Walter said. "Last time I checked, this was my store."

She whipped around to glare at Walter. "That's Mrs. Fontleroy to you."

"No, it's not. That idiot Herbert divorced *Mrs. Fontleroy.* You are something else entirely. I'd go with Vanessa if I were you. It's the politest name I have to offer."

Her eyes widened and she sucked in a breath. "Wait until I talk to Herbert about this. Poor Celia mourning her daughter and you're sitting here serving Pansy's killer cake. It's almost as if you're celebrating."

"If Carter knew who the killer was, he would arrest them," Walter said.

She gave them a smug smile. "Oh, he'll arrest her all right. I'm going to see to that."

She whirled around and stalked out of the store, slamming the front door as she went.

"You shouldn't have done that," I said. "There's no use making trouble for yourself on my account."

"Who said it was on your account? Hell, if I was interested in being bossed around by a woman, Ida Belle would be carting my manhood around in her purse."

I grinned. Walter may be love-struck, but he still wasn't a fool.

Scooter opened a side door and poked his head into the store. "Miss Morrow?"

"Please, call me Fortune."

He gave me a shy smile. "I've got your Jeep ready to go."

I glanced at my watch. "That was fast. I'm impressed."

The tips of Scooter's ears turned red and he looked down at the floor. "I'll drive it around front for you. You can check out with Walter."

"He's handy with a tool set...." Walter looked at me and raised his eyebrows.

"Still not interested."

He shrugged and added the charges to my store tab. "Never hurts to ask, although I'd already figured you for the picky sort."

"Then I guess I'm destined to spend all my time in Sinful as a single girl."

He rubbed his chin and studied me for a moment. "Maybe. Maybe not."

"You just said I was picky."

"Yep. But I figure there might be two men in Sinful who could handle a woman like you. One is myself, of course, but that would have been about thirty years ago. But my nephew—he's just the sort of man you need."

"Carter?" I shook my head. "Oh no. He's way too rigid, and besides, it would probably look bad if he dated his murder suspects."

Walter sighed. "Well, there is that. But boy it would be a sight—you two hooking up. I guarantee it would be the first time in that boy's life he couldn't make something go his way, but it sure would be fun watching him try."

"I'm genuinely sorry to disappoint you."

"Ha. You aren't sorry in the least." He rose from his stool and gestured at the front door. "Come on. I'll escort you to your vehicle so the locals don't accost you as you're leaving."

I hopped off my stool and headed to the front of the store, the conversation with Vanessa Fontleroy still rolling through my mind. As soon as I got in the Jeep, I would call Gertie and tell her I needed an emergency meeting. Pansy's missing cell phone held the answers to everything.

And I was determined to find it.

Chapter Fourteen

I clenched my cell phone and looked across the table at Marie, Gertie, and Ida Belle. Marie looked anxious. Gertie looked excited. Ida Belle looked like she was prepared for battle. I figured my own expression was a mixture of the three. We'd all sneaked over to Marie's house where we'd have a clear view of Celia's.

"Are you sure you want to do this?" I asked Ally, who was sitting in her car a block away. "I don't want you to take the risk unless you're absolutely sure."

"You've already asked me a hundred times," Ally said, "and my answer isn't going to change, even if you ask a hundred more."

"Okay, okay. I'm just a little nervous about this. Promise me that you won't push the issue. If Celia won't let you help with things or you can't access Pansy's room without getting caught, then don't attempt it. We'll figure out another way."

"I promise," she said, starting to sound a little exasperated.

"If you get a chance to go in the kitchen, try to see if anything is amiss. I mean…" I trailed off, not wanting to blurt out that she should look for bloodstains on the flooring.

"I understand," she said, her voice grim.

"We're ready over here. I'm going to put my phone on speaker and mute, so we'll be able to hear you but no one can hear us. Remember to put the phone in your shirt pocket or we probably won't be able to hear much."

"Got it. The window in Pansy's closet faces Marie's house. I'll signal when I'm in, so be watching."

I took a deep breath and blew it out. "All right. You're up."

We all peeked out the window and watched as Ally pulled up the street and parked in front of Celia's house. She reached into the backseat of her car for a casserole dish and headed up the sidewalk to Celia's front door. She rang the doorbell and a couple of seconds later, the door flew open.

"What do you want?" Celia's voice boomed over the cell phone.

"Hello, Aunt Celia," Ally said. "I brought you a chicken casserole—your favorite. Today is my day off work so I came over to help."

"My only child is dead. What can you do to help?"

"I'm so sorry, Aunt Celia. I know anything I do doesn't amount to much, but as a Christian and my momma's daughter, I can't in good conscience sit in my house all day when I know you're here suffering."

For several seconds, the cell phone was silent and I was certain we were all holding our breath.

Finally, Celia sighed. "I know we don't always

agree on things, Ally, but your momma raised you right. God knows, you didn't get any of your manners from my brother, God rest his soul. Come in, then."

"Yes!" I yelled and gave Ida Belle a high five.

"She's good," Marie said.

Gertie nodded. "Playing the Christian card always works with Celia. She's the worst hypocrite in Sinful but can't stand the thought of being exposed as such."

Ida Belle rolled her eyes. "Like it's a secret."

"Sssh," I said. "They're talking again."

"I meant it when I said I don't know what you can do," Celia said. "Between the GWs and your casserole, I have enough to eat for a week."

"I thought maybe I could do some housecleaning. Or perhaps help you pick out an outfit…I didn't know if you'd be able, that is…"

"I started going through her luggage this morning, but I didn't find anything suitable. I was going to look in her closet at some of the clothes she left behind when she moved. I thought maybe one of her old church dresses would be nice. Maybe something in pink."

"She always loved the pink," Ally said. "Do you want me to take a look? I could pick out what I think works and bring them down for you to see."

"It's nice of you to offer, but I've got no business sitting in this kitchen all day," Celia said. "I'll come with you. It will be nice to have another opinion, especially of a younger person."

"That was nice of her," I said, surprised that Celia might actually have a heart.

"Even though you're not as adept at fashion as

Pansy," Celia continued, "I suppose you can still be of some use to me."

"And she ruins it," Ida Belle said.

The voices stopped for a bit, then we heard the muffled sound of feet plodding on a wooden staircase. In one motion, we all fled the front window and shifted to the side window with a view of Celia's upstairs windows.

"The room at the back is Pansy's," Marie said. "She used to climb out at night and shinny down the trellis."

"Nice," I said. "The big one is probably the bedroom, so the smaller one to the right must be the closet."

The phone crackled with static, then Ally's voice sounded again. "I can pull out all the pink dresses for you to see. Does she still have that pink rose necklace that you got her for graduation? I think it would be lovely for her to wear it."

"I didn't look through her jewelry case earlier," Celia said. "I'll do that now while you check for dresses."

We all stared transfixed at the small square window. A second later, a hand appeared, giving us a thumbs-up.

"That's our cue," I said and motioned to Ida Belle and Gertie.

They grabbed their purses and headed for the rear of Marie's house to go get Gertie's car, which was parked a block over. A couple of minutes later, I checked my watch.

"Where the hell are they?" I asked.

Marie bit her lower lip. "Ida Belle probably should have gone for the car and picked Gertie up closer to the house. Gertie really needs to work out."

I sighed, frustrated with myself for forgetting to work Gertie's complete lack of physical fitness into my plan. "I guess we'll have to hope Ally can drag out the pink dress search."

"I'm sure she can," Marie said. "Ally is smart and capable. A lot like you. It's no wonder you're friends."

Given that Ally was currently embroiled in playing the spy, Marie's comment was a lot closer to the truth than she even realized.

Finally, I saw Gertie's Cadillac swing around the block. I felt my pulse tick up a notch as Gertie parked and they made their way to the front door.

"Keep your fingers crossed that this works," I said. "If Celia doesn't let them in, Ally may not have time to find the journal."

Marie crossed her fingers on her left hand and used her right to lift a slat of the blinds. "Ida Belle's talking," she said finally. "Celia must have opened the door."

I picked my cell phone up from the end table and held it closer to my ear, but all I could hear was the scratching and bumping of Ally moving things around.

"Are they still at the door?" I asked.

"Yes," Marie said. "They've been talking a while. Celia should have invited them in by now."

Crap!

"I found it!" Ally's voice sounded on the phone.

I fumbled to turn off the Mute button as I saw Ida Belle and Gertie shove their baked goods at the front door. Clearly, Celia's southern manners were not going to extend to friends of mine. It was a good thing no one but Carter had seen Ally and I hanging out, or she probably wouldn't have gotten past the front door, either.

Now, the problem was getting her out.

"Hurry up," I hissed. "Celia won't let them in. They're leaving."

"I'm trying, but the board won't go back down."

"Stomp on it, then knock something off the top shelf to cover the sound. Just hurry!"

I heard a loud thump, then Ally came back on the line, her voice strained. "The leg of my jeans is wedged in between the two pieces of wood."

"Well, yank it out!"

"What do you think I'm trying to do? It's not budging. Oh, God, I hear Celia coming up the stairs. Do something!"

"Call Ida Belle!" I yelled at Marie.

She grabbed her cell and dialed Ida Belle, then shoved the phone at me.

"You have to go back," I said. "Ally got the journal but her pants are stuck in the floorboard. Hurry!"

We watched out the window as Ida Belle spun around and broke into a run for the front door. Gertie's jaw dropped as she stared.

"Ally," I hissed into the cell phone. "Are you there?"

I stared up at the window, my pulse racing. What if Celia ignored the doorbell? What if she caught Ally red-handed with Pansy's journal? If Celia thought the book would mar the image she had of her daughter, she'd never let it out of her house, even if it meant finding her daughter's killer. After all, she was already convinced it was me, so from her point of view, she had nothing to lose.

I reached over to clutch Marie's arm as I saw the closet window rise up. A second later, a small square object flew out of the window and landed on the lawn in between houses.

I pulled on Marie's arm so hard, she almost fell over. "She threw the journal out the window! Call Gertie."

Marie called Gertie and shoved the phone back at me again.

"Ally threw the journal out the window," I told Gertie. "Run down the side of the house and get it and don't let Celia see you."

Gertie broke out in a run, much faster than I'd expected, especially as she was wearing a skirt and dress shoes and carrying that enormous purse of hers. As she approached the journal, she leaned to the side, still running, in an apparent attempt to scoop up the journal as a lineman would a fumble.

But for Gertie, it didn't come off quite as smoothly as it did in the NFL.

When she reached down for the journal, her giant purse swung around her shoulder and conked her square in the back of the head, sending her face-first into the turf.

"Ouch!" I yelled as Marie winced.

Not to be deterred by the small matter of slamming into the lawn at full speed, Gertie rolled over the journal, scooping it up as she went, then stumbled to her feet and ambled toward Marie's backyard, looking like a drunk running from the cops.

Marie hurried to the back door and let her inside.

I jumped back to the front window in time to see Ida Belle stomping down the sidewalk, then stopping and looking around, probably wondering what the hell had happened to Gertie, since her Cadillac was still sitting empty at the curb.

"Ida Belle, the car—" I pointed to the front of the house as Marie came hurrying back into the living room, a bedraggled Gertie limping behind her.

Marie glanced out the window, then got behind Gertie, shoving her out the front door to intercept Ida Belle. I had to give Ida Belle credit. Despite the fact that Gertie was red-faced and limping, her dress was torn, and she was toting a huge piece of sod on her purse, Ida Belle didn't even lift an eyebrow before hurrying to the car and jumping inside. She must have been hell as a spy.

I picked up the phone and held it to my ear, completely forgetting it was on speaker. Hopefully, Ida Belle's repeat call on Celia had bought Ally enough time to get loose.

"Come on you son of a—ahhhhhh!"

A loud crash followed and I yanked the phone away from my head, my ears ringing from the volume. Marie's hand flew over her mouth, and I fumbled for the Mute button before we gave the whole thing away.

"What in God's name is going on in here?" Celia's voice boomed.

"I didn't notice that my shoelace got caught in between the floorboards. When I tried to leave my foot caught. I grabbed hold of the bar to steady myself, but all I succeeded in doing was bringing the whole thing down on top of me. But the good news is, I found the pink dress with the roses that

Pansy always liked."

"Because I'm a Christian," Celia said, the aggravation clear in her voice, "I've got to assume that you mean well, but I'm going to have to ask you to leave now. I've been more stressed since you got here than I have been since I found Pansy on the kitchen floor. Between you and those two meddling women, any thoughts I had of a peaceful day are completely ruined."

"I'm really sorry, Aunt Celia. If there's anything I can do, please let me know."

"You have fulfilled your familial duty. If you really want to help, then please stay out of my house. All you've accomplished is creating more work for me."

"And finding the pink dress."

I shook my head. How Ally could sound cheerful with Celia being so rude was beyond me, but then Ally probably had years of practice. I heard the sound of muffled footsteps on the staircase again and a couple of seconds later, Ally stepped out of Celia's house.

"I'm sorry about the closet," Ally said.

"Yes, yes, just go." The door slammed shut.

Ally shook her head, then hurried down the sidewalk to her car. She'd barely pulled away from the curb before she popped back on the phone.

"Please tell me you got the journal," she said.

"Gertie got it."

"Thank God! What a mess. I would make a horrible spy."

I smiled. "Oh, I don't know. You thought quick enough to toss the journal out the window, and you can fabricate a plausible story on the spot. That bit about the shoelace was genius."

"Not really. That actually happened to me when I was in high school. I bet anything Aunt Celia remembers it too, as my mom was as aggrieved then as Aunt Celia is now."

I laughed. "That makes the story even more genius, not less."

"I like 'genius.' I'll go with it," she said and giggled.

"Did you go into the kitchen?"

"Yeah, but I didn't see anything odd. She's still got the same old linoleum floor, though, so not like there is grout or hardwood that would show staining or anything. Sorry I can't be more help on that one."

"No apologizing. Today's success is all because of you. I don't suppose you saw any sign of Pansy's cell phone?"

"I didn't get a chance to go through drawers or anything, but I'm sure the police already did that. I didn't come across it in the closet."

"Hmmm. I'll have to do some more thinking on that one then."

"I don't suppose I can risk coming to your house to read the journal with you."

"No, that probably wouldn't be a good idea, but I promise I'll call you as soon as we figure anything out."

"Sounds good. Well, before my blood pressure gives me a heart attack, I'm going to go home for a hot shower and a stiff drink. And it's not even noon. Jeez."

It took me a second to process her words and realize just how far out of the realm of normal this had been for Ally. It made me feel important and guilty at the same time. "I really appreciate what you did, Ally."

"Hey, what are friends for?"

I slipped the phone into my pocket, still smiling.

"Did she make it out okay?" Marie asked.

"Yeah."

I explained what had happened in the closet to Marie. Her eyes widened until they couldn't get any bigger, then she started chuckling.

"Oh my," Marie said, fanning her face with her hand. "Between Ally and Gertie, this entire event was a comedy of errors. Did you have this much trouble when you were helping me?"

I stared. "Ida Belle and Gertie never told you about that?"

"No, and when I've brought it up, they've always redirected the conversation."

"Ha. Probably because they exposed me to twenty levels of crazy and don't want to admit it. I tell you what—when this mess with Pansy is cleared up, we'll get together for dinner and drinks, and I'll tell you exactly how far off the normal chart your friends are."

Marie smiled. "I'd like that, but somehow, I doubt anything you say will surprise me."

"Somehow, I do too."

Chapter Fifteen

"Well, don't make us wait any longer," Ida Belle said, pointing at my hand that held Pansy's journal. "I tried to get Gertie to let me see on the way to your house, but she refused to let go of the damned thing. She drove over here with one hand and no glasses. Took out four Mayor Fontleroy reelection signs, and I think she punctured a tire."

"I did no such thing," Gertie argued.

I peered out the screen door and saw Gertie's Cadillac sitting slightly to the side. "Uh-huh. Well, you may want to call Walter unless you plan on walking home."

Gertie looked outside. "Crap."

She reached to open her handbag and pulled away the large piece of turf. I opened the front door and she tossed it onto the lawn before digging out her cell phone.

"This calls for refreshments," I said and waved them to the kitchen.

I poured iced tea for everyone and we waited impatiently for Gertie to finish making arrangements with Walter before opening the journal. Finally, I slipped the journal open and started scanning the text.

"Well, what does it say?" Ida Belle demanded.

"We were right—she went to work for an escort service," I said and flipped through several more pages. "But it looks like she didn't get along with the owner—a woman."

"Of course she didn't," Ida Belle said.

"She decided she could make more money if she went independent," I said. "Apparently, she took several of her clients with her."

"Is that allowed?" Gertie asked.

Ida Belle rolled her eyes. "You think prostitutes have a non-compete clause?"

"I doubt they have anything that they'd want to take to court," I said, "but you can bet that her former employer wasn't happy when Pansy made off with clients."

"Unhappy enough to track her down and kill her?"

I frowned. "I doubt it. More likely, the former employer is who turned her in to the IRS."

Ida Belle nodded. "That makes sense. Get rid of the competition and get the clients back without having to get your hands dirty."

"Would the IRS bother to track down the source of her income?" Gertie asked. "Or would they just do that amputated income thing that Marie talked about?"

"Imputed income," Ida Belle corrected.

Gertie waved one hand in the air. "Whatever. The question is still valid."

"Yes, and it's a good one," I said. "If the IRS attempted to track down sources, some anxious men and/or hacked off wives might have been in their path."

"So a worried customer could have killed Pansy to prevent her from giving his name to the IRS," Ida Belle said, "or she could have given the information to the IRS and they questioned the men, stirring up a potentially murderous wife."

"Exactly."

Ida Belle pointed to the journal. "Then let's get those names."

I flipped through the journal, scanning page after page of Pansy's diatribe about her unfair life and how she was due far greater things and everyone in Hollywood was keeping her down. Blah, blah, blah. It went on for a countless number of pages.

Finally, I started flipped the pages like a deck of cards, looking for a page with white space, which might signify an end to Pansy's egotistical ranting and the beginning of the information we were looking for. I finally found what I wanted at toward the end of the journal.

"Three names," I said and read them off to Ida Belle and Gertie. "Have you heard of any of them?"

They both shook their heads.

"They're not famous actors or directors," Gertie said, "but there's a lot of wealthy people in LA who aren't attached to the movie industry."

"Let's see what we can dig up on them," I said and reached for my laptop.

I typed in the first name and got a page of hits. "Mark this one off the list," I said as I clicked on the first link and scanned the contents. "He died eight months ago and wasn't married."

"It's better if we can narrow it down, anyway," Gertie said.

I nodded and typed in the second name. "Another bust. This guy moved to France six months ago with his partner—another man."

Ida Belle raised her eyebrows. "I don't even want to know."

"Last one," I said and typed.

Ida Belle and Gertie leaned across the table.

"Well?" Ida Belle asked.

"This may be our guy," I said, a stir of excitement starting in my belly. "He's a pro-am marathon runner and a plastic surgeon in Beverly Hills."

Gertie whistled. "I bet he's making a fortune...and now we know how Pansy afforded those new boobs."

"Is he married?" Ida Belle asked.

I clicked on a news article about a charity event and smiled. "Oh, yeah, and his wife comes from a politically connected family with old money."

"He's married to Maria Shriver?" Gertie asked. "I thought she was married to the Terminator."

Ida Belle rolled her eyes.

"She's not a Kennedy," I said, "but apparently the family name has some weight in California."

"Sounds like a man who has a lot to lose," Gertie said.

I turned the laptop around and showed them a picture of the skinny blonde with breasts that were way too large for her frame. "That's his wife."

"Good God. She looks like Pansy," Ida Belle said. "Do they make you go blond and get implants in order to get a driver's license over there?"

"Probably if you live in Brentwood," Gertie said, "which is where this article says they live." She reached into her handbag and pulled out a cell phone. "This is one of those disposable phones. We can call his office and see if he's been out of town recently."

"You bought a disposable phone for this?" I asked, impressed that Gertie had thought that far ahead.

Gertie shook her head. "Ida Belle and I keep a couple on hand—in case of emergencies."

I took the cell phone from Gertie, not about to ask what emergencies constituted an inventory of untraceable cell phones, and punched in the number for the plastic surgeon's office.

"Hello," I said when the receptionist answered. "I spoke with Dr. Ryan last week about possibly scheduling some work. He was supposed to call me back on Friday, but I never heard from him."

"I apologize for that," the woman said. "Dr. Ryan left Friday afternoon to attend a surgical seminar in New Orleans. He was in such a rush getting out of here that it probably slipped his mind."

"I understand. When will he return?"

"He should be back in the office on Wednesday. Would you like for me to schedule you an appointment?"

"No, thank you. I'll call back some other time." I hung up the phone, unable to contain my excitement. "He left Friday for a surgical seminar in New Orleans."

"Find the seminar," Ida Belle said, waving a hand at my laptop. "If it's being held at a hotel, there's a good chance that's where he's staying."

I did a search for medical conferences in New

Orleans but came up empty for the past weekend. Several variations yielded the same result.

"It looks like he lied about the conference," I said.

Ida Belle's cell phone went off, blasting Linkin Park across the kitchen.

Gertie covered her ears with her hands. "Why can't you have George Strait, like everyone else?" she yelled.

Ida Belle waved a hand at her. "It's Genesis," she said and answered the call.

Gertie and I waited while Ida Belle nodded and exclaimed, and by the time she got off the phone, we were ready to burst.

"Genesis got the gig working on Pansy. She asked to see the body this morning so she'd know what kind of supplies to bring."

"Did she ask how Pansy was killed?" I asked.

Ida Belle shook her head. "She didn't have to. There were two purple handprints on Pansy's neck."

Gertie whistled. "Strangling usually means it's personal."

"Or professional," I said. "Remember, Celia was upstairs so the killer needed to be quiet."

Ida Belle raised an eyebrow.

"Occupational hazard," I said.

"Hmmm," Ida Belle said. "Not a pleasant thought but a valid one. But given that our chief suspect is in the state for no apparent reason, that doesn't seem to apply. Surely, if he'd hired someone to kill Pansy, he would have made sure he stayed in LA and in front of as many people as possible."

"That's true if we assume she's dead at his

hands, but what if his wife hired someone?"

Gertie nodded. "Those families with old money hate scandal, although they're usually guilty of the biggest ones."

"But surely," Ida Belle said, "if his wife had hired a killer, she would have made sure he was front and center as well."

"Unless she wanted him to be blamed for the murder," I pointed out. "Maybe she found out he was chasing Pansy to New Orleans and decided to kill two birds with one stone."

Ida Belle gave me an appreciative look. "You have an excellent criminal mind."

"It's all speculation," I pointed out. "Remember, we only have his receptionist's word that he came to New Orleans. But we don't know for sure that he even came here or that he's still here. He may have changed his mind and gone to Fiji instead, figuring it was all too big a mess."

"I would have opted for Fiji as well," Gertie agreed.

"So if I were a rich plastic surgeon, what hotel would I stay at in New Orleans?" I asked.

"The Ritz-Carlton," Ida Belle and Gertie answered in unison.

I tapped in the Ritz-Carlton into the laptop and dialed the hotel on Gertie's disposable phone.

"Hello, this is Jean with Copy Express," I said to the front desk clerk. "I have a package for Dr. Ryan, but the person who took down the address has awful handwriting. I wanted to make sure this is the right hotel before I drive over there."

"Yes," the desk clerk said in her crisp and professional voice. "Dr. Ryan is staying with us.

You can drop off the package at the front desk and we'll see that it's delivered to him."

"Great. Thanks." I hung up the phone. "Jackpot."

Gertie bounced up and down on her chair, clapping her hands. "We are so smart."

"Yeah, but what do we do with the information?" Ida Belle asked.

Gertie stopped clapping and frowned. "I hadn't gotten that far."

"We really should give this information to Carter," I said.

Gertie shot a worried look at Ida Belle. "Somehow, I don't think he's going to take it all that well."

"I don't think so, either," Ida Belle agreed. "And what do we really know? Maybe this Dr. Ryan is four foot eleven and has hands like a ten-year-old girl. If he's not our killer then we've exposed a whole lot of our business to Carter for no good reason."

"Maybe we should go to New Orleans and take a look at his hands," Gertie suggested.

"No way," I said. "If Ryan is the guy, we're putting ourselves at risk if he sees us. For all we know, he could have studied up on people in Sinful, and none of us look like the five-star-hotel type. If he's already strangled one woman to keep her quiet, what would stop him from strangling a couple others?"

"But if it's clear that it's not him," Ida Belle argued, "then we don't have to give up trade secrets to Carter and nothing has been lost but our time and for some of us"—she rolled her eyes over at Gertie—"probably a bit of dignity."

"I'm not sure my purse is going to make it," Gertie said, completely oblivious to Ida Belle's insult. "That turf really did a number on the clasp."

"Carter told me not to leave town," I said, not about to admit that Ida Belle's plan had merit, especially in the "keeping off Carter's radar" column.

"We went to Mudbug on Saturday," Gertie pointed out.

"He didn't catch us going to Mudbug," I said. "I can't be in trouble for something he doesn't know about."

"Exactly," Ida Belle said with a broad smile.

I slumped back in my chair, knowing I was defeated. Gertie and Ida Belle were going to check out that man's hands, whether I went with them or not. And darn if my own curiosity hadn't gotten the better of me. I really wanted to see his hands, too.

If his hands could fit around a neck, and he looked like he had the strength to strangle Pansy, then we could turn the suspect over to Carter. Granted, he'd be madder than a hornet about our interference, but he wouldn't be able to argue over the results.

"Fine," I said. "We'll check out this doctor's hands. But we will not engage him in any way." I pointed my finger at both of them. "Is that clear?"

"Crystal," Ida Belle said.

"Scout's honor," Gertie said and threw a peace sign.

Somehow, I wasn't encouraged.

Chapter Sixteen

It was just after two o'clock when we climbed out of Gertie's Cadillac in the parking garage down the street from the Ritz-Carlton. We started down the sidewalk, going over our plan one last time.

"I will go to the front desk with the package," I said, holding up the brown-wrapped empty box that Gertie had assembled for our mission. "I'll say I need a signature for it, and if we're lucky, Ryan will be in his room."

"I'll wait near the elevators, and when I see him come down," Gertie said, "I'll signal to Fortune to leave before the desk clerk can point her out."

"I'll be standing near the front desk," Ida Belle jumped in, "pretending to wait on a friend, and will get a good look at his hands when he steps up to the desk."

"No improvising," I said. "If we cause trouble in this hotel, they won't hesitate to call the cops."

They both nodded, but I still wasn't convinced.

Just before we arrived at the hotel, I pulled a ball cap out of the backpack Ida Belle had supplied me with and put it on, shoving my ponytail underneath it. Then I donned reflective sunglasses and popped a piece of bubble gum in my mouth. I took a deep breath and gave them a nod before heading down the sidewalk and into the hotel.

I'm not much of a luxury-living person, but I have to admit, the hotel lobby was nice with its fancy furniture and huge plants. A middle-aged, uptight-looking woman with her hair pulled up in a bun narrowed her eyes at me as I approached the front desk. Clearly, she'd already decided I had no business in the hotel.

"Got a package for Dr. Ryan," I said, pasting on a bored expression.

"I can take that," she said and reached across the counter.

"Gotta have a signature," I said and popped my gum.

She moved her hands back and winced, then reached for the phone. "Let me see if I can reach him."

I backed against the counter and chomped on my gum, catching sight of Gertie as she slipped into the hotel and headed for the elevators. Ida Belle followed a couple of seconds later and hovered near the entrance, waiting for my signal.

A couple of seconds later, the desk clerk spoke. "Dr. Ryan. There's a package delivery for you at the front desk."

She put her hand over the phone and looked at me, still frowning. "He's not expecting a delivery."

I pointed to the label. "Says Dr. Ryan at the Ritz-Carlton right here. Do you have two Dr. Ryans staying here?"

"No, but—"

"Then he's the one."

"Perhaps if you could tell me who the package is from..."

"No can do. They just hand me the packages and I deliver 'em. I don't care who they're from as long as I get paid."

She gave me a scathing look and removed her hand from the phone. "I'm sorry, Dr. Ryan, but the delivery service doesn't know the origin of the package. I would accept it for you, but they're requiring your signature."

A couple of seconds later, she hung up the phone. "He'll be here in a few minutes."

"Cool." I pushed off the front desk, touched the brim of my hat to signal Ida Belle, and strolled across the lobby, stopping to finger a plant. "Hey, are these real?" I yelled back at the desk clerk.

I swear, I could feel her sphincter tighten. "Yes, please don't touch the plants. You could damage them."

"Whatever you say, lady." I let go of the plant and walked a little farther across the lobby and closer to the exit. The front desk clerk seemed relieved the farther away I got. So far, the plan was working.

Ida Belle strolled across the lobby and stopped a couple of feet from the front desk. The desk clerk looked over at her, the same putrid expression on her face. "Can I help you, ma'am?"

"I'm waiting for my friend."

"I can call her room if you'd like and tell her you're here."

"She hasn't checked in yet. Damned woman's always late."

The desk clerk looked uncertain. "We have some

comfortable seating in the middle of the lobby," she said and waved a hand in the direction of some furniture that looked as uptight as the desk clerk and not even remotely comfortable.

"I got the hemorrhoids and didn't bring that doughnut thing that lets 'em hang," Ida Belle said. "I'll just stand here unless you got a problem with that."

The desk clerk blanched. "No, ma'am," she said, clearly resigned to an afternoon of dealing with crazy people.

I looked over at the elevators, where Gertie was positioned behind a giant banana plant. Thank God her dark green dress blended in with the leaves, because it was a suspicious place to hang out. The desk clerk's gaze began to wander in that direction. I looked over at Ida Belle, hoping she'd notice the clerk's wandering eye and Gertie's stalkerish hiding choice and come up with a distraction, but she was busy reading something on her cell phone.

I was just about to head over to the desk myself, when an older couple came through the front entrance, a valet following them with a cart that contained so much luggage I wondered if they were moving into the hotel. The woman started ordering the clerk around before she even got to the desk, waving her hands in the air as if conducting a symphony. Every finger on her hands sported a very large and extremely tacky piece of jewelry, and I would have bet anything it was all real, just like the strip of fur hanging around her neck—in June.

Something large and white flickered at the edge of my vision range and I turned to the left to see a man shuffling across the lobby wearing a fluffy white spa robe and matching slippers. When my eyes ventured up from the wardrobe and to his face, I knew we were in trouble.

It was Dr. Ryan.

I started to bolt out the front door, but somehow that didn't seem fair as Ida Belle and Gertie hadn't even noticed that our plan had gone awry. As he walked toward Gertie's hiding place, she peered out from behind the banana plant and even from across the lobby I could see her eyes widen in panic.

I started a mental prayer that she didn't do anything stupid, but I didn't make it past "Please" before she'd made the point moot.

I wasn't sure if she tried to signal us that he was in the lobby or slow him down long enough for me to escape, but she managed to accomplish both. She bolted out from behind the banana plant—at least, she attempted to. Her ever-present, incredibly large handbag got caught on an edge of the planter, which normally would have stopped her in her tracks, but since she'd launched out as if she were on fire, she managed to pull the entire plant over as she bolted.

The plant and Gertie crashed to the ground in a sea of flying leaves, dirt, and some random cursing, coming to a stop at Dr. Ryan's feet. I should have taken that opportunity to flee, but I stood frozen, clutching the empty box. One glance at Ida Belle, who was stiff as a post, told me no ideas were racing to her mind, either. The clerk stared for several seconds, then hurried from behind the desk.

Immediately, Dr. Ryan bent over to help up Gertie, who was flailing, scattering the mass of leaves and potting soil like a cartoon character. Her eyes were clenched shut, probably full of dirt. As the doctor bent over, Gertie, who was grasping for anything solid, caught on to the sash of his robe and attempted to pull herself up. Unfortunately, the sash loops on the robe weren't designed to bear the weight of panicking seniors with forty-pound handbags, and they tore completely off the robe, exposing much more of Dr. Ryan than we'd come to see.

The desk clerk emitted a strangled cry and the older woman at the front desk, who'd turned around to see what all the commotion was about, screamed and fell onto the marble floor in a dead faint.

Ida Belle and I broke out of our trances at the same time and ran across the lobby to help up Gertie, who now had the bottom of the doctor's robe in a death grip and refused to release it. Clearly panicked, Dr. Ryan pulled on the robe, desperately trying to cover himself, yelling at Gertie to let go. When I reached down for her, she blinked several times and opened her eyes on the way up. Unfortunately, the way up was straight up Dr. Ryan's full frontal and she followed the desk clerk's example and let out a startled cry.

Finally free of Gertie, Dr. Ryan pulled the robe around himself and sprinted for the elevators. The desk clerk recovered some of her composure and glared at Gertie. "I ought to call the police," she said.

"And I ought to sue," Gertie countered. "That's a horrible place for a plant. I could have broken a hip."

Ida Belle stepped over to Gertie. "Are you all right? I didn't know you'd checked in already."

Gertie waved a hand in dismissal. "I'm not

staying in a hotel that allows attack plants and naked men in the lobby. Take me to a Hilton."

Ida Belle nodded and pulled Gertie, whose vision still appeared to be off, across the lobby and out the entrance. The desk clerk looked over at me, her frustration and disgust clear.

"I'll just come back later," I said. "Naked men aren't part of my job description. I may file a sexual harassment complaint over this."

I gave one final glance at the front desk, where the older man was trying to help Mrs. Liberace up from the floor, then hustled out of the hotel before the desk clerk made good on her word and called the police.

Outside the hotel, I immediately crossed the street away from Ida Belle and Gertie, just in case anyone from the hotel was watching, and hurried between the buildings until I was a block over. Then I walked the rest of the block and doubled back to the parking garage. Because I'd taken the long route, Ida Belle and Gertie had beat me to the car, where Gertie was blowing through an entire container of baby wipes, trying to get the dirt off her face. She'd started with her eyes and now looked like a raccoon with a reverse mask. At least Ida Belle had insisted on driving.

"Let's get the hell out of here before someone sees us," I said.

Ida Belle put the car in gear and punched it, tires squealing as we exited the parking garage. I sank down in the backseat so that no one could see me until we merged onto the highway. Between the potting soil and the baby wipes, Gertie's face was now so streaked with mud she looked like she'd been on a three-day jungle tour.

"Well, it didn't exactly go as planned, but at least we know that the good Dr. Ryan could have strangled Pansy. His hands were big enough and in a rage, his strength would have been doubled or tripled."

"I didn't see his hands," Gertie said, "but he had small feet. I don't even have to tell you what they say about small feet."

"No, you don't have to tell us," Ida Belle agreed. "We saw that firsthand."

"I guess that's something even plastic surgery can't fix," Gertie said.

Ida Belle nodded. "But on the upside, at least that was one thing that wasn't in your grasp."

Gertie fanned herself with her hand. "Lord, just the thought makes me blush! It's bad enough I got a full-face view of the thing. Even with dirt in my eyes, it was quite startling."

My eyes widened. Given my profession, I was hardly up for a sexual prowess award, but given the number of years Gertie had on me, I couldn't imagine something so unimpressive being startling.

"But, ah....surely," I said, "you've...um, seen one before?"

Gertie shot me an indignant look. "I've seen plenty in my day, but it's been a number of years since I've had one so close to my face. You've been around Sinful long enough to see the male population selection."

I smiled. It was a valid point.

"All discussion of full-face frontals aside," Ida Belle said, "we have a problem."

My smile vanished. "Yeah. We have to make

sure Carter gets this information, and preferably before Dr. Ryan and his big hands leave town."

Gertie's eyes widened. "You're going to tell him about today?"

"No!" I couldn't even imagine the horror. "If there's a God, only the three of us, Dr. Ryan, the desk clerk—who is quite possibly scarred for life—and that woman who passed out and her husband will ever know about today."

"The whole thing was almost worth it," Ida Belle said, "just to see that old bitty hit the floor. But you're right. Carter needs to know about the journal and about Dr. Ryan's suspicious proximity."

"We could leave the journal in his truck or mailbox with a note," Gertie suggested.

I sighed. "It's not that simple. In order for the journal to be introduced into evidence at a trial, someone has to testify as to how they obtained it and from where. In this case, Ally would have to admit to knowing about the hiding place and taking the journal."

Gertie raised her eyebrows. "You really have been watching a lot of television."

"I wish that were the case, but unfortunately, that little bit of legal requirement has prevented the Justice Department from pursuing certain cases, especially when people like me gathered the evidence."

"Certainly you're allowed to testify, right?" Ida Belle asked.

"No. The agency can't afford to lose capable agents every time we run across evidence of a crime, especially when it's usually not pertaining to the mission I'm on. We turn over what we have, hoping they can find another way to prove it, but there's not much more we can do."

"That blows," Gertie said.

"And it puts Ally in a position I didn't want her in." I sighed. "I guess I didn't think this through very well."

"Don't you worry," Gertie said. "We'll figure something out."

I nodded, but I knew that the only way for Dr. Ryan to show up on Carter's radar was if Ally confessed to petty theft.

Not exactly the kind of thing great friendships were made of.

⁓⁓⁓

About five miles outside of Sinful, Ida Belle pulled over to the side of the road and I assumed my reentry position—in the trunk. Not wanting to risk someone seeing me leaving town, we'd agreed that on the way out of town and back in, it would be best for me to hide in the trunk. It was only seven miles or so, which you'd think wouldn't have been that big of a deal, especially for someone in my shape. Unfortunately, Gertie's ancient Cadillac had more battle wounds than a Roman gladiator, and presented some unique challenges.

For starters, half of the trunk bottom was rusted out, and I had to stay on one side of the car or risk falling through onto the street. Then there was the small matter of the trunk lid...which wouldn't stay closed. At first, Gertie held it down by securing it to the bumper with a bungee cord. But sometime between the squirrel incident that took out the front bumper and this morning, something had transpired that had eliminated the back bumper completely.

When she'd arrived, the trunk had been taped shut with duct tape, but for the sake of simplicity, I was now scrunched into one side of the trunk, clutching a rope that held down the trunk. Every time Ida Belle hit a bump on the crappy road leading to Sinful, the trunk, the rope, and I flew up about a foot.

It felt like I'd been bumping around in the trunk for hours when I heard a police siren. I prayed that it wasn't for us, but every second that passed, the sound got louder. Finally, the car swerved to the right and I heard the crunch of gravel, indicating that Ida Belle had pulled over on the shoulder of the road.

"Just stay cool!" Gertie yelled.

"Stop yelling! Ida Belle yelled.

Carefully, I inched forward and peered through the broken keyhole. It was my worst nightmare confirmed—Carter climbed out of his truck and walked toward the Cadillac.

"Good afternoon, ladies," he said. "You want to tell me where you've been?"

"Not particularly," Ida Belle said.

"Let's try again," he said. "Tell me where you've been."

"I can't see that it's any of your business," Ida Belle said.

"Yeah," Gertie threw in. "We're not breaking the law."

"Now, that's debatable, because this car is probably in violation of something, but I pulled you over because I suspect you know and/or are involved in the disappearance of Miss Morrow."

"Fortune's disappeared?" Ida Belle's pretend

shock was impressive.

"Maybe she was kidnapped by aliens," Gertie threw in.

"If anything," Deputy LeBlanc said, "she was confiscated by two old ladies who seem to take pleasure in causing me grief."

"I have no idea what you're talking about," Ida Belle said.

"Who are you calling old?" Gertie retorted.

I shook my head.

"Then if you two aren't up to anything," Deputy LeBlanc continued, "You won't have any problem opening the trunk."

"Do you have a warrant?" Ida Belle asked.

Good girl!

"Do I need one?" Deputy LeBlanc asked. "Because I can keep you sitting here on the side of the road while I get one. It might take a couple of hours, and I imagine we'd all be pretty hungry by then, not to mention needing to use the restroom, but if that's the way you want to play it..."

"Okay," Ida Belle said. "But Judge Poteet is having liposuction and telling everyone he's in Cancun. He'll come back white as a sheet and jiggling a bit less, so I doubt anyone's going to buy it. And Judge Aubry is at his mistress's house in Mississippi, but he told his wife he's going to a law conference in Baton Rouge."

Nice!

For several seconds, only silence carried back to the trunk, and I smiled, imaging the look of aggravation and dismay that Deputy LeBlanc was likely wearing.

"Fine," Deputy LeBlanc said finally. "I want the

two of you to go home, but you haven't heard the last of this. If I find out that you transported Miss Morrow outside of Sinful, there's going to be hell to pay."

"Yeah, yeah," Ida Belle said and started up the car.

I let out a sigh of relief, but it came a second too soon.

Chapter Seventeen

The weak floorboard gave way and I dropped out of the trunk and onto the shoulder of the road, collapsed in a heap. Ida Belle, completely unaware that the trunk had finally given way, tore off from the shoulder of the road, scattering a wave of gravel and dirt over me.

I covered my head with my arms to protect myself from the onslaught, then a shadow fell over me. I looked up at the clearly angry Deputy LeBlanc.

"I don't know whether to throw you in jail or a mental institution."

At the moment, I wasn't sure about the correct choice, either.

"Is this multiple choice?" I asked. "If so, is there a third option?"

He extended his hand down to me and pulled me upright. "Yeah, option three is where I arrest all three of you and let you sit in jail until Judge Poteet is recovered from his secret liposuction or Judge Aubry's mistress gets bored and makes him leave."

A screech of brakes echoed back at us, and we looked over to see the Cadillac slide to a stop, then begin backing up.

Deputy LeBlanc shook his head. "I'll say this for them—they won't desert a sinking ship."

Ida Belle stopped the car a couple feet away from me, then she and Gertie jumped out and rushed over. Deputy LeBlanc glanced at them, then did a double-take at Gertie's dirt-streaked face.

"Are you hurt?" Ida Belle asked as Gertie walked around me, lifting my arms and inspecting me for injuries.

"I'm fine—just a little dusty."

"Your hands are bleeding," Gertie said and turned my palms up where I could see.

"It's just a couple of nicks. I'll be fine."

"You could have been killed!" Deputy LeBlanc exploded. "What would have happened if you'd fallen through that trunk when Ida Belle was doing sixty down this highway?"

"Oh," Gertie said, "my car hasn't done sixty in well over a decade."

Deputy LeBlanc glared. "Even at twenty miles an hour, she could have been seriously hurt." He pointed his finger at Ida Belle and Gertie. "Now, I've already determined that the two of you either have a death wish or have lost all good sense, but what floors me is how you've managed to convince someone new in town to go along with your shenanigans."

"Oh, well, that was easy," Gertie said.

Ida Belle elbowed her. "We didn't convince her to do anything but take a ride to the antique shops in Mudbug."

"Uh-huh." Deputy LeBlanc didn't look the least bit convinced. "Then why is her face so dirty?" He pointed at Gertie.

"Those shops are filthy," Gertie said. "I reached for a pillow on top of a shelf and brought a whole stack of old quilts along with their dust down on me. I tried to clean it off with baby wipes, but it streaked."

He narrowed his eyes. "If you're not up to something, then why was Miss Morrow hiding in the trunk?"

I threw my hands up in the air. "Because you told me not to leave town, but I'm tired of being physically assaulted with iced tea and verbally assaulted by every dimwit in this town. There are a *lot* of dimwits."

"That's true."

"She has a point."

Ida Belle and Gertie spoke at once.

"The truth is," Gertie said to Deputy LeBlanc, "we knew you'd get your panties in a wad if you found out Fortune left town, especially with us. But she needed a break from this place and by God, we saw that she got it."

Deputy LeBlanc raised his eyebrows. "Panties?"

Gertie waved a hand in dismissal. "Boxers, briefs...heck, you may go commando for all we know. Apparently, that's popular these days."

"Uh-huh. So if I call these antique shops, they'll verify that you were there today?"

"How the heck should we know?" Ida Belle asked. "The clerks in those stores are as old as their merchandise. I can't vouch for their memory."

"Are you going to arrest us, or what?" Gertie asked. "If so, I need to call Marie and tell her to record the movie on Lifetime for me."

He stared at each of us, taking several seconds apiece to study our faces, but he was up against a trained professional and two of the best retired liars I'd ever met. We weren't giving up a thing.

Finally he blew out a breath. "It would be better on you to tell me what you're up to, because I'm going to find out."

"We were just taking a break," Ida Belle said.

Gertie nodded. "Enjoying some of the summer greenery."

I choked back a laugh and nodded.

"I give up," he said. "Get in that car and get back to Sinful. I want *all* of you in the seats." He looked directly at me. "And no more leaving Sinful until I've sorted this Pansy mess out. Understand?"

"Loud and clear," I said and hurried to the car.

I looked back at Deputy LeBlanc as we drove away, certain we'd just made things much worse for Ally.

❦

It took me an hour to get Ally on the phone. In an effort to relax, she'd gone fishing, which for Ally translated into sleeping in her boat, so she hadn't heard her cell phone ringing. I gave her a brief rundown of our findings in Pansy's journal and our trip to New Orleans, leaving out the more dramatic details.

"I'm so sorry, Ally," I said. "I never wanted you involved, but I don't see any way around it if we want the evidence to stand up in court."

"It's all right," she said. "I figured everything would come out eventually."

"That's not necessarily true," I said. "It doesn't have to come out unless it goes to court. We need to arrange to speak to Deputy LeBlanc in private. I think I can convince him to keep this quiet until absolutely necessary."

"I don't want you in any more trouble than you already are," Ally argued. "I'll tell Carter it was all my idea."

"No. I won't let you do that."

"Well, I'm not about to let you do it. You're already a suspect and the bottom line is I'm the one who stole the journal and it was my idea to do so. Carter doesn't need to know I had help."

"At least let me go with you. You shouldn't have to do this by yourself. After all, you did it for me."

"I don't know...won't people wonder if you and I stroll into the police department and ask to talk to Carter?"

I frowned. She had a point.

"Hold on," I said and explained the situation to Ida Belle and Gertie.

"We can meet in the back room at the General Store," Ida Belle said promptly. "I'll call Walter and set it up."

"Won't Walter mind us using his store for sordid business?" I asked, not bothering to argue with the "we" part of her statement. I knew arguing with her was futile.

"We do it all the time," Ida Belle said and punched in Walter's number on her cell phone.

I didn't even want to know what kind of sordid business Ida Belle conducted in Walter's store on a regular basis, so I just waited until she finished the phone call.

"He said you can come now," Ida Belle said. "Tell Ally to take her boat and go in the back entrance. We can enter by the front. Walter will call Carter when you're both in position."

"Did you get all that?" I asked Ally.

"Yep. I'm heading that way. Make sure you bring the journal."

"Right," I said and hung up the phone. "Gertie, can your purse handle transporting the journal to the General Store?"

"It's on its last leg, but I think it can handle the journal."

"Good, then I'll need one more ride in your car. Marge's Jeep doesn't have a top and I don't want to risk another demented citizen attack on my way to the store."

Gertie stuffed the journal into her handbag and we headed out.

We were the first to arrive at the store and my curiosity was piqued when Walter escorted us to a back room without question, then said, "Let me know when to call for Carter."

He closed the door behind us and I looked over at Ida Belle.

"He's not going to ask why we're meeting like this?"

"Heck no," Ida Belle said. "Walter learned a long time ago that it was better not knowing what we were up to."

Gertie nodded. "Knowing means you might be called to testify."

"Just how often are the two of you involved in things that might require the other to testify?"

"Well, I don't really have a number," Ida Belle said vaguely.

"Probably once a week or better," Gertie said.

"Every day if you take into account that we're running moonshine as cough medicine."

"But Walter sells the cough medicine in his store," I pointed out.

"Yes, but he's never drunk any," Gertie said. "That way, he can always say he didn't know."

Ida Belle nodded. "Plausible deniability is a useful thing in Sinful."

I shook my head. "You people should be in DC. You could give them a run for their money."

Ida Belle waved a hand in dismissal. "Politicians are boring. Most of them are only average intelligence, if that, and their motives are clearly defined by self-interest. No challenge really when someone's walking around wearing their weak spot on their fake smile."

She had a point.

The door opened and Ally stepped inside. Walter poked his head in after her.

"You ready for that call?"

"We're ready," I said. No sense putting it off any longer.

Walter ducked back out and Gertie pulled the journal from her handbag and handed it to Ally.

"Are you sure we're ready?" Gertie asked. "Don't we need to get our stories straight first?"

"No!" Ally said. "I don't want Carter even knowing you helped. There's no sense all of us being in trouble."

"But—" I began.

"No arguing," Ally said.

I smiled. "I don't think I've ever seen you this forceful."

She smiled. "You never saw some of my

arguments with mother—especially before she moved to the assisted living center."

"Ally's mother is a real piece of work," Gertie agreed. "We always said Ally's dad died so that he could get away from her. It was the only place she couldn't readily follow him. Sorry, Ally."

Ally laughed. "It's not the first time I've heard it, and unfortunately, I have to agree. My dad was a really nice, docile, quiet man. I never understood why he married my mother, who was his exact opposite in every way."

Ally's smile faded. "I talked to Mom today. You guys should know Aunt Celia's sister came to visit her. She told mom she's not attending the funeral."

"Wow," I said. "She must really be holding a grudge against the mayor if she won't even come to her own niece's funeral."

"Did she say why?" Gertie asked.

Ally shook her head. "If she did, mom's not telling. I came right out and asked how she could do that to Celia. Mom said some things are too painful to face, no matter what good manners call for."

"Hard to believe she loved the mayor so much it still hurts," Ida Belle said.

"Especially when she made off with the better part of his money," Gertie said, "but then, she always was a strange one. She and Celia are cut from the same cloth that way."

"Nice to know there's two of them," I said.

"Ssshhhh," Ida Belle said. "I think I hear Carter…yep, that's definitely him."

"Showtime," Gertie said and looked at Ally. "Take a couple of deep breaths and get centered. If he asks you anything that you don't want to answer, pretend to be confused. It works every time."

Ida Belle rolled her eyes. "It works for you because he thinks you're dim-witted. He's not going to give Ally the same leeway."

"I don't need leeway," Ally said. "The truth is the best defense."

Ida Belle sighed. "Oh, to be young again."

The door flew open and we all spun around to face it. Carter took one step into the room and frowned.

"Oh man," he said, "there is no way anything good is happening here."

Then he locked in on Ally and sighed. "Don't tell me they've got you involved, too? This is so disappointing."

Gertie opened her mouth but Ally stepped on her foot and inched toward Carter. "Actually, I'm the one who got them involved."

Carter raised one eyebrow. "This ought to be good."

"It's not good, but it's relevant to your investigation," Ally said, and told Carter about Pansy's ranking list from high school and its hiding place in her bedroom closet.

"So I figured," Ally continued, "Pansy being Pansy, she probably hadn't stopped keeping score, and if she brought it with her from LA, then it would be a good list of who might want her dead."

"Why would some man want Pansy dead because she graded his sexual prowess?" Carter asked. "How would he even know?"

"I don't think the guys would know, but if you remember, Pansy specialized in 'attached' men."

"Oh," Carter said. "And you think one of those

men might be afraid Pansy would tell?"

"Wouldn't you be if you'd slept with Pansy?"

Carter blanched, slightly raising my opinion of him. "Definitely."

"So I thought maybe a scared man or his angry wife would be a prime suspect."

He sighed. "I see. And if I had another suspect, then I might not arrest Miss Morrow, which seems to be the current push among some of Sinful's more vocal residents."

Ally nodded. "Fortune had no reason to kill Pansy, and I don't believe for a moment that she did. But some people will not rest until they see her behind bars."

Carter frowned. "Do all of you really think I'm foolish enough to let a lynch mob dictate how I do my job?"

"No," Ida Belle said. "But if you don't find the real killer before the mob spins out of control, you may not have a job."

His expression didn't change, but I saw the tiny tic in his jaw and knew that it was a truth he'd gotten around to already, even though he wasn't about to admit it.

"Anyway," Ally said. "All of that was to say that I went to Aunt Celia's house and pretended I wanted to help her choose an outfit for Pansy so that I could look in the cubbyhole and see if Pansy had hidden a list there. And she had." She handed him the book.

He took the journal and looked at me, Ida Belle, and Gertie. "And I'm supposed to believe that the three of you had nothing to do with this?"

Ally turned around and glared at us, and we all

put on our most innocent-looking faces. Carter knew better but as usual, he had no evidence.

"So if you have to arrest me for stealing," Ally said, "then go ahead. I understand."

"I'm not going to arrest you," Carter said. "Yet. But you realize what kind of position you've put yourself in if this goes to trial? Why didn't you just tell me your suspicions and let me look for the journal?"

Ally shook her head. "If Aunt Celia got even an inkling of an idea that something like this existed, she would have burned it."

"Even if it meant destroying evidence against the person who murdered her daughter?" Carter asked.

"Aunt Celia is a bitch, but a practical one. Nothing can bring Pansy back, but something like this would mar Aunt Celia's community standing. Everyone knows what kind of person Pansy was, but as long as it's only gossip, Aunt Celia can ignore it and no one would dare mention it to her."

Carter didn't say a word, but I could tell he didn't disagree with Ally's assessment of her aunt.

"I'm not sorry for what I did," Ally said. "And if I had to do it all over, I'd do the same thing. I have no problem telling the truth in court—about now or back then. It's about time people in Sinful start dealing with reality and stop couching every word in misplaced politeness."

"Bravo!" Gertie said and started clapping.

Carter's lips quivered and I knew he was struggling not to smile. I didn't even bother trying. He looked away from Ally and over at the three of us.

"So I guess the big question is," he began, "if

Ally did all the thieving and plotting, then why are you three present for the confession?"

"Because we came across some information that fits with what Ally told you," Ida Belle said.

"What kind of information?" Carter asked.

"Pansy owed the IRS a ton of back taxes from working as an escort—a very highly paid one from the size of the bill."

"And you found this out how exactly?" Carter asked, his ears beginning to redden.

"We're not saying," Ida Belle said, "but I'm sure you can verify it all with the IRS. The escort part is in the journal."

"You read the journal?" Carter exclaimed, on the verge of explosion. "What part of 'stay out of my investigation' do the three of you refuse to understand?"

"There was no point giving you the damned journal if it didn't say anything relevant," Ida Belle said. "We would never let Ally confess to stealing unless it was worthwhile."

He stared up at the ceiling and blew out a breath. I wasn't sure if he was praying or counting to ten.

Finally, he looked back down. "So since you arranged this secret confession, I guess that means the journal contains something worth going to jail for?"

Ida Belle nodded. "One of Pansy's big customers is a plastic surgeon, and he's been in New Orleans since last Friday. His receptionist thinks he's at a conference, but there are no medical conventions of any type in New Orleans this weekend."

"It's very suspicious," Gertie threw in.

Carter narrowed his eyes at us. "Tell me I did not

catch you coming back from New Orleans earlier."

Ida Belle rolled her eyes. "You did not catch us coming back from New Orleans. We already told you where we were."

"Uh-huh. So I'm to believe that Ally snatched this journal, gave it to you three, and you read it and then went antique shopping?"

"Yep," Ida Belle said, "that's it exactly."

"You didn't do anything else?" Carter asked, not buying it for a second.

"We did eat hot dogs on the way," Gertie said. "Those big ones from 7-Eleven. I don't think we told you that part. And I had strawberry soda and Lay's potato chips. I wanted a candy bar, but *some* people have been harassing me about my fitness, so I abstained."

"I had yogurt and mineral water," Ida Belle said.

"I—" I started to throw in my two cents, but Carter held up his hand to stop the barrage.

"I don't care," he said. "Half of what comes out of your mouths is nonsense. The other half is lies. I tell you what I'm going to do. I'm going to lock the three of you up in jail overnight. Then maybe you'll think twice before you go against a direct order from a law enforcement officer."

Chapter Eighteen

"What are we charged with?" Ida Belle demanded, hands on her hips and glaring.

Carter smiled. "I don't have to charge you with anything to detain you for questioning."

"You can't keep us there indefinitely," Ida Belle argued.

"No, but I can keep you there long enough for me to get a good night's sleep and a whole day of investigating without having to follow up on you three." He waved a hand at the door. "After you."

Gertie's eyes widened. "But Ida Belle and I were going to have a *Walking Dead* marathon tonight."

"You can improv it in the cell," Carter said.

"I'm going to assume," Ida Belle said drily, "that's not a dig at our age."

"Take it however you'd like," Carter said, "as long as you take it to cell number two. Junior Petrie's working off a two-day drunk in cell one."

I waited for the comeback, the argument, the whatever needed to happen to get us out of this, but for the first time since I'd met them, Ida Belle and Gertie seemed stumped. They simply nodded and started heading for the door. I sighed and fell in line behind them.

As Ida Belle reached for the doorknob, Carter's cell phone rang. He answered and I could immediately tell it wasn't good news.

"What the hell do you mean—you've got to be kidding me!"

He shoved the phone in his pocket. "Looks like you're off the hook. Apparently, something has caused the air-conditioning unit at the sheriff's department to catch fire."

Sure enough, a second later, we could hear the whine of a fire engine.

"Oh my," Gertie said. "What caused the fire?"

Carter smirked. "If I weren't standing here looking at you three, you would have been my first bet for it. Sheriff Lee thinks it was a raccoon."

I frowned. "You let raccoons carry lighters?"

"Only on Mondays," Gertie said and patted my arm.

"Regardless of how it happened," Carter said, "I can't hold you there in June with no air-conditioning. Looks like you're off the hook once more. But this is my last warning—if I catch any of you poking into my investigation again, you're going to sit there until I catch the perpetrator, even if we all sweat to death."

He pointed a finger at Ally. "That includes you, which is highly disappointing because I've always given you credit for being smarter. I want you to think long and hard about the company you're keeping. It may shorten your freedom and/or life expectancy."

He whirled around and stomped out of the back room. We all looked at each other and I let out the breath I'd been holding since he said he was taking us all to jail. Sitting in jail meant legal paperwork. If Director Morrow saw his niece's name pop on anything, he'd go ballistic and I'd be flipping burgers somewhere in the Midwest.

"That went well," I said.

Ally frowned. "Is he always so disgruntled when you help him? You'd think he'd be a little more grateful that we just handed him a prime suspect."

Ida Belle laughed. "Keep thinking that way, Ally, and you'll be on Carter's permanent shit list along with the three of us."

Ally grinned. "At least I'd be in good company."

"Got that right," Gertie said and gave Ally a high five.

"I owe you—big time," I told Ally.

"You don't owe me anything," she said. "That's what friends are for."

I smiled, still amazed that it had taken traveling across the country under an assumed name and with a price on my head for me to find friends who were worth claiming.

"I hate to break up this Folgers coffee commercial moment," Ida Belle said, "but Ally needs to get out of the store before someone sees her. I know you might end up testifying, but until that becomes reality, there's no use for you to put yourself in Celia's warpath."

Ally nodded, then threw her arms around me, surprising me with a quick hug. "We're going to get you out of this," she whispered, then with a wave to Ida Belle and Gertie, she slipped out of the storeroom and back into the store.

"Such a nice girl," Gertie said and sniffed. "If I'd

had a daughter, I would have wanted her to be just like Ally."

"Not me," Ida Belle said. "All that niceness might rub off. Can't afford for that to happen."

Gertie rolled her eyes. "Imagine the horror."

I grinned. "Let's get out of here. I've still got gravel dust in my hair and it itches."

Ida Belle peered out the door. "Coast is clear."

We hustled out of the storeroom and into the store. At the same time, Walter came hurrying in from the back door, wiping his hands with a rag.

"Got held up at the dock," he said.

"Did you see the fire?" I asked.

He raised his eyebrows. "Is that what all the noise is about?"

"Yeah," I said. "Apparently, a raccoon set fire to the AC unit at the sheriff's department. I'm surprised you didn't see a commotion since it's only a couple buildings down from here."

He frowned. "Thought I smelled something burning, but sometimes there's a burning smell when Sammy's curing hides."

I cringed. Yuck.

"Thanks for letting us use your room," I said and stuck my hand out. "I'm sorry to put you in the middle of things."

Walter hesitated for a moment, then shook my hand. "All I did was unlock a door and make a phone call."

"Well, I still appreciate it," I said.

Ida Belle and Gertie gave Walter a wave and we started out of the store. I reached up to push my bangs to the side and a familiar smell wafted by. I lifted my hand back up—the hand that Walter had shaken—and took a big whiff.

Gasoline!

I whipped my head around and stared at Walter, who gave me a wink and went back to stocking. I waited until we were back in Gertie's car before exclaiming, "Oh my God. Walter set fire to that AC unit."

Neither Gertie nor Ida Belle seemed even remotely surprised.

I stared. "You already knew?"

"Suspected," Gertie said, twisting around in the passenger's seat to look at me.

"But how would he even know Carter was going to arrest us?" I asked.

"He left the storeroom phone on speaker," Ida Belle said, "so he could hear the conversation. I saw the light as soon as we walked in the room."

"You asked him to do that?"

Ida Belle shook her head and pulled the Cadillac away from the curb. "I don't ask Walter to do anything like that. If I knew he was going to listen, then he wouldn't be able to claim lack of knowledge on the subject matter."

"She doesn't want to owe him," Gertie said, which was an explanation I bought more readily.

"Then why did he did he set the fire if not for Ida Belle?" I asked, completely confused.

Gertie pursed her lips. "That's the interesting part. I don't know for certain, but I'm going to guess that he did it because he likes you and was worried."

"If you like someone, you help them change a flat tire or bring them food," I said. "There's a huge gap between those types of things and criminal mischief."

Gertie nodded. "I think you remind him of someone." She inclined her head toward Ida Belle.

"Oh." I slumped back in my seat. In a strange way, it made sense.

Gertie had commented earlier that she would have liked Ally as a daughter, if she'd gone that route. I hadn't thought of it at the time, but if Ida Belle had a daughter, she'd likely be more like me.

I wished Walter hadn't gotten involved, but in the pit of my belly was a small warming glow. It was nice to have people care about me—people who tried to help without being asked or offered anything in return.

I smiled and said a silent prayer that Carter never found out his uncle was working for the dark side.

I showered until the hot water ran out, then spent another ten minutes under the cold, trying to invigorate my exhausted body and mind. It had been an incredibly long day, but I knew if I fell asleep this early, I'd be awake in the middle of the night, and that was something I hated.

Time seemed to pass so much slower when it was dark outside, and everything seemed starker. It was a slow crawl into depression.

I knew why I felt that way. I wasn't as out of touch with my emotions as people accused me of being. I just didn't wear them on the outside like an extra layer of clothing, nor did I dwell on them like well-meaning people sometimes suggested I do. "Sit with the pain." "Find your center with your memories." "Take a pill."

Depending on whom I was talking to—well-meaning coworker, CIA shrink, or New Ager who was part of an undercover operation—everyone seemed to think I needed to do something different with my feelings. I always resisted the advice. The way I'd handled things had worked fine my entire adult life.

At least, I thought it had been working.

Then I'd come to Sinful, and I started wondering if my profession, and all the lifestyle requirements that came along with it, had allowed me to remain stuck in an emotional rut, always pointing to professional success as proof of how well I was doing. But what did I really have to show for my life, except a bunch of completed missions that I could never talk about?

I threw on yoga pants and a T-shirt and trod barefoot downstairs to fix up some dinner. Unless the house caught fire, I was in for the night and determined to get some sleep. As I walked through the living room, I glanced out the front window into the fading sunset, wondering if I would see Sheriff Lee parked across the street on his horse—or even worse, on my own front lawn.

My eyes narrowed. I was definitely under surveillance, but it wasn't by horse and it wasn't Sheriff Lee. I flung open the front door and stalked down the driveway to Carter's truck. He saw me cross the street and lowered the stack of papers he'd been reading, then shoved them into an expandable file on the passenger's seat.

"Seriously?" I asked. "You couldn't arrest us, so you're going to spend the night stalking me?"

"It's surveillance when the police do it," he said, looking aggrieved.

"Since I'm innocent of the crime you're investigating and you know it, that's debatable."

He sighed but didn't respond. I took a good look at him and realized he was even more exhausted than I was, which stood to reason. He'd been on twenty-four/seven duty for days, with a murderer on the loose, half the population of Sinful angry at him for not arresting me, and a good chunk of his time wasted chasing me, Ida Belle, and Gertie around. And none of that included the investigation he was conducting.

I wave of empathy washed over me. I'd been where he was far too many times in the field. Some missions were in and out. Others seemed to drag on endlessly and without decent food or sleep. It took weeks for me to recover every time I returned home.

"Are you hungry?" I asked.

"What?" He looked confused, but I suppose it was a strange question.

"Have you eaten?"

He held up a coffee and a half-eaten protein bar, and my empathy ticked up another notch.

"I'm about to heat up a chicken casserole from Francine's. Why don't you come in and get something decent to eat?"

A wistful look passed over his face before he shook his head. "That wouldn't be appropriate."

"Why not? You're here to make sure I don't go on a killing spree, right? If you're sitting in my kitchen, I can't attempt to kill anyone but you. Besides, maybe the great citizens of Sinful will think you're questioning me or searching my residence and cut you some slack."

He tilted his head to the side and studied me for several seconds.

"What's in it for you?" he asked finally.

I threw my hands up in the air. "Maybe I'm just being nice. Contrary to what you and other people might believe, I can be a very nice person. Maybe I feel sorry for you because in a way, you're in as bad a position as I am, and neither of us has done anything to be there. Maybe I'm afraid if you don't eat some of the casserole, I'll consume the entire thing and have to spend the next ten years jogging it off."

His lips quivered for a second, then finally the smile broke through. "Well, I suppose people might think I'm finally coming down on the Yankee criminal."

"Hey, it's a win for everyone."

He pushed open his truck door and stepped out, clutching the expandable folder under his arm. I figured it must be Pansy's file if he wasn't even willing to leave it in his truck. Of course, he might also figure I would get him back into the kitchen, then have Ida Belle and Gertie steal the file out of his truck. I have to admit that for a second, it had crossed my mind, which probably made me a bit less nice than I'd claimed.

He followed me inside and back to the kitchen, where I directed him to the breakfast table. He slid into the corner chair and placed the folder on the table next to him.

"You want a beer?" I asked.

"More than anything in the world, but I can't have one."

"Right, you're working. Soda? Iced tea?"

"I don't suppose you have root beer, do you?" he asked, looking like a hopeful ten-year-old.

"Actually, it's my favorite. I took the last four two-liters at the General Store." I grabbed the root beer out of the refrigerator and poured two tall glasses.

Carter took a huge gulp of the root beer and gazed outside at the muddy bayou, slowly swirling its way to the Gulf of Mexico. I pulled out the casserole, cut off two big hunks, and put them in the toaster oven to reheat.

"You know," he said, still staring out the window, "when you grow up in a place like Sinful or even just visit one, you don't think any awful things happen."

He turned from the window to look at me as I slid into the chair across from him. "I mean, nature is a bitch, so there's hurricanes and tornados, and a lot of the professions here have dangerous elements, but that's all part of normal life."

"But murder isn't," I said quietly.

"Not usually."

I nodded. "I remember thinking when I walked through town the day I arrived that probably the only time something was killed here, it was eaten, then stuffed."

"Or peeled and fried." He gave me a small smile. "Yeah, that used to be the case."

"What do you think happened?"

He shrugged. "The simple answer is time. People are crueler—more desensitized to things that would have shocked them ten years ago—and the dark secrets that people kept years ago seem to be bubbling up."

"So you're saying good southern manners prevented people from poking into others' business in decades past, but now, people are less likely to cover up or even ignore questionable behavior?"

"Yeah, pretty much."

"So you think Pansy's past finally caught up with her?"

"I'm not at liberty to discuss an ongoing investigation, especially with a suspect."

I rolled my eyes. "That's a yes. Did you check into Dr. Ryan?"

He sighed. "You're not going to quit asking questions, are you?"

"Hey, my freedom is on the line here. You can't blame me for asking."

He frowned and studied me for a couple of seconds. "No, I guess if I were in your position, I'd be asking as well, so I'll throw you a bone. The New Orleans Police have detained Dr. Ryan on my request. I will take a trip there tomorrow morning to question him, but I don't expect much to come of it."

"Why not?"

"Because he asked for a lawyer before they ever got him out of the hotel."

The buzzer sounded on the toaster oven and I got up to retrieve the casseroles. I wasn't the least bit surprised that Ryan had lawyered up. I would have done the same thing in his position and with his pocketbook. But at least if he was in custody for suspicion of murder, Carter shouldn't have any trouble getting a look at his phone records.

I sat one of the plates in front of Carter and took my seat across from him again. The first bite made me sigh.

"If I lived here permanently," I said, "I'd have to be towed around on a flatbed trailer."

Carter smiled. "Francine has a gift."

"So does Ally. Wait until you taste the peach cobbler she made a couple days ago."

"One of my favorites," he said and took another bite of casserole. "You and Ally have gotten to be friends, huh? I wouldn't have put the two of you together."

"Why not?"

"Partly because of the ex-beauty queen thing and Ally's past with Pansy. Partly because Ally's a people person and librarians are usually more introverted."

"And partly because I'm from north of the Mason-Dixon Line?"

He grinned. "Partly."

"The beauty queen thing was overblown by my mother," I said, giving him my regular cover story. "It was her dream, not mine. And it's true, I am an introvert. People tend to annoy me as long as they're talking, and sometimes when they're not."

"But yet, you took up with Ida Belle and Gertie—the two worst influences in Sinful—on the very day you set foot in town."

"I know, but they needed my help. I figured, 'Here are these two nice old ladies and their friend being accused of murder'—why shouldn't I pitch in?"

"You got taken."

I grinned. "I know that now, but how was I supposed to know it then? They seem so innocuous."

He nodded. "And then the next minute you're wearing nothing but a trash bag while fleeing the Swamp Bar."

"There is that, but still, I don't regret helping them. Marie is a really nice woman and now, she's finally free to have a decent life without the shadow of her husband's disappearance hanging over her head."

He studied me for a moment, then nodded. "It could be that you're just a nice, naive woman, but I doubt it. I get the impression you enjoy being in the thick of the action."

I gulped down some root beer, trying to formulate a good reply. Of course I enjoyed being in the thick of the action. My entire life was centered on being in the middle of things, but the real Sandy-Sue probably wouldn't have made a single decision I'd made since I arrived in Sinful.

"I guess I've been cooped up in the library for too long, and I really like that *Law & Order* show."

"So do I, but you know what the difference is? I'm actually a law enforcement officer. You're a civilian, and when civilians try to handle police business—especially when it involves things like murder—they often become the next victim."

He wasn't wrong. I knew firsthand what happened when amateurs attempted dangerous jobs. I'd seen the body bags. But the amateur title didn't fit me. Granted, I wasn't law enforcement, but I wasn't an average civilian, either. Of course, Carter didn't know any of that, so it was only proper that he bring up such things in an attempt to keep me out of harm's way.

But on some level, it still rankled me.

A big part of me wanted him to know just how capable I was. Just how close a match we truly were in the "alpha soldier and dangerous human being" department.

"Don't worry," I said. "I have no intention of becoming a victim."

A murder victim or a railroaded suspect victim.

I just didn't specify all that to Carter.

"So what's your story?" I asked, trying to change the subject.

"What do you mean?"

"You know—why did you come back to Sinful after your military tour, what are your career plans—the usual stuff."

He raised one eyebrow. "You checking me out, Miss Morrow?"

I felt a light blush creep up my neck and mentally cursed. Of course, I wasn't interested in Carter in the way he was implying. I was living here under an assumed identity and would be gone like a whisper of wind as soon as things cleared up for me on the professional front. But I'd be lying if I said I wasn't attracted to him.

I imagined most women with a pulse found him attractive. He was probably the hottest guy I'd ever met in person, and he was oozing with the whole alpha male thing. But Carter managed to make it seem more about being a hero and less about his ego, unlike the alpha males I worked with at the agency.

"No. I'm not checking you out. I try not to date men who might arrest me for murder. But I can't ask about the case, and my life before now was the most predictable thing on earth. I just started watching television recently, so I can't chat about current events, famous people gossip, or sports."

"You just started watching television? Were you being held hostage or do you have some religious objection to the device?"

Well, that was a loaded question. I actually had been held hostage on more than one occasion, but I was going to assume the question was tongue-in-cheek and answer accordingly.

"I'm more of a reader," I said, then prayed that he didn't ask me what I liked to read.

"I guess that makes sense, you being a librarian. What sort of stuff do you read?"

Crap.

My mind went on autopilot, sifting through a lifetime of knowledge and trying to lock on to something that would answer his question but that I could back up with intelligent answers if he had more questions. Unfortunately, the only thing I really knew was my job.

"I mostly read technical stuff—you know, how things work. And I like historical nonfiction."

That was mostly true. I read the specs on new weapons on a regular basis, and since I'd been in Sinful, I'd started reading some from Marge's impressive collection of historical weapons books.

"Sounds riveting," he said. "No wonder you're asking about my life."

I shook my head. "Has anyone ever told you that you have a really big ego?"

He grinned. "Not to my face."

"Well, there's a first time for everything."

"I didn't," he said.

"You didn't what?"

"I didn't return to Sinful when I left the military—at least, not right away."

"Oh. Where did you go?"

I expected him to say "the beach" or "the mountains" or whatever variation of locale that he found interesting, but I was wrong.

"Indiana," he said.

"Okay, I'll bite. Why Indiana?"

"Because that's where Lance Corporal Stephen Taylor's widow and newborn son live."

I lowered my fork, a heavy feeling settling over my chest. "He was in your unit?"

"He was under my command."

My heart clutched and I took a long, slow breath. No matter the situation, if you were in charge of another human being, and they died on your watch, you felt responsible. I'd been fortunate that only two agents had died during joint missions. And even though I couldn't have done a single thing to prevent what happened, I knew I would carry the weight of their deaths with me forever.

"I'm sorry," I said finally.

He nodded. "Me, too. So I spent some time there, doing what little I could to help, then I came home. After everything I'd seen and done, I needed grounding. Sinful may be strange, but it's still home."

Grounding.

It was a concept I was familiar with in theory but couldn't say that I'd experienced myself. Maybe because after my mother's death, my life contained no stable ground to return to.

"You look confused," he said.

"No," I said, breaking myself out of my trance.

"I was just thinking that I don't really have a place to ground."

"Why not?"

"My father died when I was young, and we always lived in big cities with no community feel. I went away to college and moved to another state for work. When my mother died, I suppose I lost the last thing that really tied me to New England."

"So why don't you leave?"

I frowned. "I guess because the life I have back there, as stark as it may be, is the only one I know."

"Maybe it's time to learn something new."

His words were still hanging in the air when his cell phone rang. He answered it and his face immediately shifted from personal to professional, and he didn't look happy. After shooting out a couple of clipped answers, he rose from the table and picked up the folder.

"I appreciate the meal, but I've got to run," he said.

"What's wrong?"

"Mark Bergeron just confessed to murdering Pansy."

My mouth dropped. "Who is Mark Bergeron?"

"A guy I went to high school with. Married Joanie, a local girl." He shook his head. "I thought they had it together."

"Oh." My mind flashed back to the couple I'd seen arguing on their way out of the Catholic Church the night Pansy was murdered.

"You've got a look on your face like you know something," Carter said.

"No. I mean, I think that's the couple I saw arguing Friday night at the beauty pageant rehearsal."

"Did you hear what they were arguing about?"

"About some woman who was calling Mark. Joanie didn't appreciate it."

"Did they say this woman's name?"

"No. Just that she was recently back in town, and Mark swore he hadn't had anything to do with her since high school and wasn't going to. Ida Belle said he was one of Pansy's many conquests."

Carter sighed. "I would never wish anyone dead, but for the life of me, I don't understand why people like Pansy exist. She caused more trouble in this town than Ida Belle and Gertie could ever dream of, and the difference in her case was that the intentions were never good. I thought when she left, it was over."

"Apparently it was...until she came back."

"Yeah. I'm sorry to leave in the middle of dinner, but I have to go arrest a man I've been friends with since we were babies."

I followed him to the front door and watched as he crossed the street and got into his truck. I'd never seen someone look so defeated.

Chapter Nineteen

As soon as he pulled away, I raced back to the kitchen and called Ida Belle and Gertie to fill them in on the development. They said they'd check their network and come over to my house as soon as they knew something. Apparently, their network was faster than DSL because they were at my front door ten minutes later.

"That was fast," I said as I let them in.

"One of the Sinful Ladies is Joanie's aunt. She's been over at Joanie's house with Joanie's mother for the last two hours. Joanie is beside herself."

"Of course she is," I said. "Her husband just confessed to murder."

"But that's just it," Gertie said. "Joanie is insisting that Mark couldn't have done it. She says they left their daughter at her grandmother's for the night so they could hash out the Pansy problem. They fought for a couple of hours, then Mark drank a six-pack of beer and passed out watching television."

"He could have sobered up enough by midnight to kill Pansy," I pointed out.

Ida Belle nodded. "True, except that when Joanie

gets mad, she can't sleep. So she turned on the house alarm and went to the kitchen to bake. She has a clear view of the front and back doors from the kitchen, and the only panel for the alarm is next to the front door."

"So he's lying?" I asked. "Why?"

"The only reason I can figure is to protect someone else," Ida Belle said.

The obvious answer hit me at once. "His wife."

Gertie nodded. "That's what we figure."

"You guys know her," I said. "Is Joanie capable of this?"

"Anyone is capable of murder," Gertie said.

Ida Belle sighed. "I think she means is she physically capable of this particular murder, and the answer is I'm not sure."

"Pansy had a good thirty pounds on Joanie," Gertie pointed out.

"Thirty is being charitable," Ida Belle said. "But sometimes the lanky ones are strong."

"True." I was one of those strong lanky ones. "And as mad as she was, that would have made her stronger."

"We have to *do* something," Gertie said, looking more distressed by the second.

"Actually," I said, "I don't think we have to do anything. I mean, at least not about Mark. That part will fix itself."

"How?" Gertie asked.

"Because the first thing Carter will ask Mark to do is describe how he killed Pansy so that he can take a statement."

"And Mark won't know Pansy was strangled because the police never released that information,"

Ida Belle said.

Ida Belle's cell phone rang. She took the call and immediately, her expression shifted to worried. "We've got to get over to Marie's. Something is happening at Celia's."

We jumped in Gertie's car, me flat on the backseat, and Gertie practically drag-raced the two blocks to Marie's house. She parked around the corner and we hurried down the block, staying in the shadows of the hedges and away from the dim glow of the streetlights. I could see the faint outline of Sheriff Lee's horse standing on Celia's front lawn.

When we got to Marie's house, we slipped into the backyard, where Marie was already waiting to let us in the back door.

"What's going on?" Ida Belle asked. "I saw Sheriff Lee's horse in the front lawn."

"I don't know," Marie said. "I was in the living room watching television when I heard screaming coming from next door. I grabbed the phone and called the police."

"Someone's-killing-me screaming or angry screaming?" I asked.

Her eyes widened. "It sounded like angry screaming to me. I mean, there were cuss words, and it sounded like someone was throwing glass. Oh my God. What if I was wrong?"

Gertie patted Marie's arm. "Don't worry, honey. Not even Celia has the balls to cuss someone out while they're trying to kill her. I'm sure it's something else."

Ida Belle nodded. "You need to go find out what."

"Me?" Marie shook her head. "I'm not good at this sort of thing."

"Well, you better get up to speed," Ida Belle said, "if you expect to join the SLS. We tend to specialize in this sort of thing."

Marie sighed. "What am I supposed to do—knock on the door and ask what's wrong?"

"Exactly," Ida Belle said. "Tell Celia you're the one who called the police and you want to make sure everything is all right or see if there's anything you can do to help. Celia loves people attempting to serve her."

Marie didn't look remotely convinced, but she allowed Ida Belle to shove her out the door and trekked across the lawn to Celia's, looking back every couple of steps.

"You sure she can do this without passing out?" I asked.

Ida Belle nodded. "That damned husband of hers convinced her she wasn't capable of anything. I aim to change all that. She's a smart woman and can do a whole lot more than sit in this house, knitting and baking."

I couldn't argue with Ida Belle's intent, especially as I'd already heard plenty of stories about Marie's deceased husband, and none of them good.

A stream of light appeared in front of Celia's house, signaling us that someone had opened the front door. I crossed my fingers that Marie was able to get anything out of the surly Celia. A minute later, the light disappeared and a couple of seconds later, we saw Marie heading back to her house.

She hurried through the front door, her cheeks

red and breathless with excitement. "Someone broke into Celia's house," she said.

"She was robbed?" I asked.

Marie shook her head. "They tore up Pansy's room—literally tore it up. The drawers are pulled out of the dresser. Everything was pulled out of the closet. The mattress has been cut."

"What in the world for?" Gertie asked.

"Somebody's looking for something," I said.

Ida Belle nodded. "Maybe Ally isn't the only person who knows about Pansy's scorebook habit."

I looked over at Marie. "Did she say what time the break-in happened?"

"She'd been home all day until an hour ago, so sometime in the last hour."

Gertie looked relieved. "That puts Mark and Joanie in the clear. Mark was already down at the sheriff's department trying to convince Myrtle to call Carter so he could confess, and Joanie's mother and aunt were with her at her house."

Ida Belle frowned. "But that puts Fortune on the hook."

"Why would Fortune want to steal Pansy's scorebook?" Gertie asked. "She didn't sleep with Pansy."

"And Joanie already knows that Mark did," Ida Belle pointed out. "Whoever broke in is probably someone whose wife doesn't know and he doesn't want her to know."

"But is he our murderer?" I asked. "Or just some poor guy worried that someone will find the scorebook and air his dirty laundry?"

"That's a good question," Ida Belle said and sighed. "Logical or no, nothing is going to stop people from accusing Fortune of the break-in."

"Actually, I'm good," I said. "I spent the past hour eating dinner with Carter."

They all stared, and Ida Belle raised her eyebrows.

"There's an interesting development," Ida Belle said.

"Not so interesting," I said, not wanting them to get the wrong idea. "I saw him parked across the street for stakeout and went over to talk to him. He looked exhausted and frustrated and all he had was a protein bar and coffee. I had Francine's chicken casserole and cobbler and I felt sorry for him, so I invited him to eat."

"Is that all you invited him to?" Gertie asked, smiling.

"Of course! Look, it's my fault he had to sit out there, so I figured it was the least I could do."

"It wasn't the least you could do," Ida Belle said, "but I'm not sure it gets you a pass, either."

"Why not?" I asked. "If the deputy is not a solid alibi, who the heck is?"

Gertie cut her eyes over at Ida Belle, a worried look on her face. Ida Belle blew out a breath.

"We weren't going to tell you," Ida Belle said, "but that accusation Celia's cousin made in Francine's on Sunday has picked up some momentum."

I frowned, trying to remember everything Celia's cousin had spewed out on me that day, then I sucked in a breath. "People think I'm sleeping with Carter?"

"*Some* people think that," Gertie said. "But not anyone with a brain."

"Unfortunately," Ida Belle said, "people without a brain make up the bulk of Sinful."

I felt my heart drop. "I made things worse when I invited him in, didn't I?"

Gertie bit her lower lip.

"Maybe," Ida Belle said.

Gertie stared at her.

"Okay, probably," Ida Belle corrected. "Foster, the man who lives across the street from you, is the nosiest person in Sinful. I'm sure he's stayed glued to his front window ever since this mess with Pansy started up."

"But there's still Dr. Ryan," Gertie said. "Once Carter latches on to him, all the pressure about Fortune should disappear."

I shook my head. "I don't think so. Carter told me Ryan is being detained by the New Orleans police until he can get there tomorrow to question him."

"Then if Dr. Ryan is in jail," Gertie asked, "who broke into Celia's house?"

Ida Belle frowned. "That is a damned good question."

Marie tried to insist that I stay at her house for the night, not wanting me to be without an alibi, but when I pointed out that spending the night next door to Celia's would probably increase suspicion rather than reduce it, she had to agree. Then Gertie and Ida Belle broke out into an argument about who, between the two of them, was more a more believable alibi. I wasn't about to wade into that mare's nest, as I figured the honest answer was neither.

Finally, I solved the problem by telling them all that I intended to sleep in my own bed and if they wanted to play armed guard, then they could all do it at my house. Given that mine was the only house with enough bedrooms and baths to host everyone in their own space, the argument ceased.

We stayed up until almost midnight, trying to make sense of everything that had happened, but it was no use. Dr. Ryan had been the perfect solution, but now, everything seemed so messy and disjointed. One of the Sinful Ladies called Ida Belle around ten to say that Carter had released Mark, but neither of them was talking. I figured Carter caught on pretty quickly that Mark wasn't the murderer, but I also figured his attempted confession had only drawn attention to his wife as a suspect, even though neither of them could have broken into Celia's house.

It was a ragged, disappointed crew that had finally called it a night and headed upstairs to bed. Unfortunately, my mind wasn't near as tired as my body and sleep didn't come. I tossed and turned for a while, then tried reading, but ultimately, I gave up and headed downstairs about one a.m. for a glass of warm milk.

Bones, who was sleeping on a blanket in his old spot in the corner of the kitchen, didn't even stir as I poured the milk and popped it in the microwave. But as I pressed the button to stop the timer before the buzzer went off, he jumped up from his bed— far more quickly than I thought possible—and raised his nose in the air and sniffed.

I froze and watched as he inched out of his bed and stuck his nose in the crack of the back door and sniffed again. Then he looked up at me and scratched the door with one paw and whined.

"Sssshh." I patted his head, hoping it would keep him from barking, and lifted one of the blinds to peer outside.

At the side of the lawn, right where the light from the porch began to fade away, something moved. My pulse leapt. Whatever it was, it was big. Plenty of small things might be moving around back there, but the only thing large enough to cast the shadow I'd seen was a human.

Not wanting to waste time going upstairs for my pistol, I grabbed a knife from the counter and gently pushed Bones away from the door, telling him to stay and be quiet. Apparently, the hound understood what I asked because he sat next to the door and leaned against the wall.

I slid back the deadbolt, eased open the door, and slipped outside, figuring that if whoever was lurking in the bushes was paying attention, they'd see me coming outside and take off. And that's exactly what happened.

He shot out of the bushes, scattering branches and leaves as he went, and ran down the side of the house to the front. I vaulted over the porch railing and took off after him, certain no one in Sinful was going to beat me in a footrace, even though I was barefoot and running with a butcher knife.

The side of the house was pitch black, but I sprinted down it, lifting my knees high just in case tree roots were exposed. I burst onto the front lawn and did a quick scan to find my target. Two houses up the street, I caught sight of someone running at the far edge of the street lights.

I pivoted left and dashed across the front lawn, not realizing until I streaked by that Carter was parked at my curb. I glanced as I passed and saw his eyes widen, but I didn't slow my pace, even when he yelled at me to stop. I pushed my legs harder and rounded the corner at the end of the block, expecting to be on top of the intruder.

Then I screeched to a halt.

No way, I thought as I scanned up and down the street, but as far as I could see, nothing moved. He couldn't have gotten an entire block ahead of me. Only a cheetah and maybe an Olympic athlete could have pulled away from me like that.

Which meant that he was hiding somewhere close by.

I was about to cross the street and start checking the row of hedges surrounding the elementary school when I heard footsteps pounding behind me. I turned around in time to see Carter slide to a stop next to me.

"What the hell do you think you're doing? Jesus H. Christ! Half this town already wants me to arrest you, and here you are running down the street, half-naked and carrying a butcher knife. Things like this can buy you seventy-two hours at a psych ward, which now that I think of it, isn't a bad idea. At least I could get a good night's sleep again without worrying that this town is going to string you up in town square."

I looked down at my boxers and tank, sans bra. "Okay, the half-naked thing is nothing new between us and quite frankly, I've given up worrying about it. But are you seriously going to tell me you didn't see the guy I was chasing?"

His eyes narrowed. "What guy?"

"Someone was lurking around my backyard. I couldn't sleep, so I was in the kitchen getting a drink and saw him at the edge of the lawn."

"So instead of calling the sheriff's department, you decided a better idea was to chase him down with a kitchen knife?"

"It's a really big knife and if you'd stop holding me up, I might get the chance to use it. He's got to be hiding here somewhere."

Suddenly, a car engine roared to life halfway up the block and peeled away from the corner, tires screeching away from us.

"Damn it!" I said. "He's getting away."

Chapter Twenty

The car was running without headlights and the street light at the end of the block was conveniently burned out, so it was impossible to determine make or model. I took off running back to my house, leaving a stunned Carter standing on the corner. Seconds later, I heard him running behind me.

When I reached my house, I ran to lift the garage door and glanced back in time to see Carter running toward me. As he passed the hedges that bordered mine and my neighbor's lawns, someone darted out of the bushes and tackled him on the front lawn.

I let go of the garage door and ran toward the hedge, where Carter and his attacker were rolling on the lawn. Then a second figure jumped out of the bushes and hit the tumbling pair with some kind of stick. I heard a loud burst of cursing and immediately recognized the voice.

"It's Carter," I yelled as I rushed over. "Stop!"

As I reached the heap, Marie chose that moment to burst out the front door with Bones and a spotlight.

And it was a direct hit.

The light settled on Carter and Ida Belle as if

they were on stage. Except in this act of the comedy of errors, Ida Belle's robe was twisted around her head and she was thrashing about while giving us all a clear view of her camouflage underwear with "Protected by Smith & Wesson" printed across them. Some of her hair rollers had fallen out and one of them was stuck right in the crack of the camouflage.

Carter jumped up as I reached down to pull the robe off of Ida Belle's head. Bones ran over and, apparently mistaking Ida Belle for a bush, lifted his leg and started peeing. I grabbed her shoulders and pulled her up from the ground as Marie hurried over, illuminating all of us with the spotlight.

"We didn't know it was you, Carter," Gertie said, holding a rolling pin and sporting Hello Kitty pajamas.

I choked back a cry as Carter looked over and got his first clear look at his assailant. His complete and utter dismay was priceless. Ida Belle straightened out her robe and shook her arm where Bones had gotten her. A roller flew off the sleeve and stuck to the hound dog's ear.

"Damn dog," Ida Belle muttered as she retrieved her roller.

"We thought someone was attacking Fortune," Gertie explained.

Marie nodded. "We were trying to help."

Carter threw his hands in the air. "And it never occurred to *any* of you to call 911? I don't know whether to be happy that you're all in one location so you're easier to watch or worried that your collective IQs seem to drop in each other's company."

"Well, you don't have to be insulting," Gertie said. "We wouldn't have to take such actions if there wasn't a homicidal maniac running loose."

Carter raised an eyebrow. "Says the woman who just assaulted a law enforcement officer with a kitchen implement."

"Why are you watching me, anyway?" I asked. "You've got a perfectly good suspect sitting in jail in New Orleans, waiting on you."

Carter stiffened and his jaw flexed. "Ryan's in the wind."

"What?" Gertie, Ida Belle, Marie, and I all yelled at once.

Pro-am marathon runner. The details of my Internet search on Ryan came crashing back.

"Keep it down," Carter said. "There was a mix-up at the police station and Ryan was released. No one has seen him since."

"His stuff is still at his hotel room?" I asked, starting to worry. If Ryan had seen me somewhere in Sinful and made me as the delivery person at the Ritz-Carlton on Monday, he might think I was in on things with Pansy.

"His wallet with all his credit cards, cash, and license are still at the police station," Carter said. "And the rest of his things are still in his hotel room. He won't get far."

"He could be here in Sinful for all you know," I said. "He could have been the one in my bushes."

Carter narrowed his eyes at me. "Why would he have any cause to know you, much less stalk you?"

Ooops.

No way was I telling that story.

"Maybe he heard the local gossip," I said.

"Uh-huh," Carter said, not buying it for a minute. Finally, he sighed. "You know what—whatever it is, I don't even want to know. I should, but I simply can't work up the energy. If any of you has an ounce of sympathy, you'll get back inside that house and stop running outside with weapons."

He whirled around and stalked back to his truck, glaring at all of us as he pulled away.

"I don't get it," I said as I watched his taillights disappear around the corner. "Why is he still watching me? I can see putting on a show for the locals during daylight hours, but I know he doesn't think I did it. Why spend the night in his truck?"

"I could be wrong," Gertie said, "but I'm going to guess it's because he's trying to protect you."

"And himself," Ida Belle said.

"True," Gertie agreed. "You're both on the hook at the moment."

I frowned, not sure how I felt about Carter looking out for me.

I was pretty sure I'd been more comfortable as a suspect.

Tuesday passed without incident, unless you took into account the thirty-six hang-up calls I received, the rotten eggs in my mailbox, and the burning pile of cow crap on my front porch. I'd totally fell for that one and now, my only tennis shoes were on the back porch, drying out from their visit with the water hose. Ida Belle had watched the entire escapade without saying a word, which should have clued me in that something was amiss, as usually she had something to say about everything.

Ida Belle, Gertie, and Marie had taken turns "sitting" with me, as they called it.

Babysitting was more accurate, although I felt more like a caged animal. Ida Belle had tapped all her sources, but no one had seen hide nor hair of Dr. Ryan. He hadn't returned to his hotel and his receptionist was vague about when he'd be available for appointments. I figured the New Orleans police had been in contact with her and at the moment, she was probably even more confused than we were.

By that evening, Ida Belle and I were all pacing my living room while Gertie started on her sixth roll of knitting yarn, not a single original idea among us. At Ida Belle's insistence, Marie had headed home with Bones to keep an eye on Celia's house.

"There's got to be something we can do," Gertie said for the hundredth time. "I feel like we're just sitting here, hoping Carter doesn't have to arrest Fortune."

Ida Belle stopped pacing and glared at her. "Don't you think if there was something we could do, we'd be doing it?"

"Well, we need to think of something," Gertie said. "Pansy's funeral is tomorrow. That will only turn up the heat."

For once, Ida Belle didn't have a smart aleck reply, and although she was trying hard not to let on, I could tell she was worried. She set off pacing the length of the living room again and was on her third pass up when her cell phone rang. Gertie and I both froze and waited as Ida Belle issued clipped one-word answers, then disconnected.

"The GWs are having a private mourning at the

Catholic Church tonight," Ida Belle said, looking excited. "Only the GWs and Celia's family are invited."

"And this makes you happy, why exactly?" I asked, not understanding her obvious glee.

"Because Celia's house will be empty," she said. "Whoever broke in there the other night didn't get what he was looking for."

"Because we already had it," I said. My pulse ticked up a notch.

"Had what?" Gertie asked. "I wish you two wouldn't talk in code."

"The journal, you woolly-headed old woman," Ida Belle said. "Ryan might go looking for the journal."

"What makes you so certain it's Dr. Ryan?" Gertie asked. "More than a handful of Sinful men have been worried since Pansy got back in town."

"But how many of them can get away from Fortune in a footrace? The short answer is none."

Gertie frowned. "Do you really think he'd be stupid enough to break into Celia's house again?"

"He was stupid enough to pay Pansy to have an affair," I said.

"True," Gertie agreed, "but what would it gain him to have the journal now? He's already wanted for questioning for Pansy's murder. I'm sure they contacted his wife, so that cat's out of the bag, assuming it was ever in."

"He's a rich Beverly Hills plastic surgeon," Ida Belle said. "He probably thinks his expensive LA attorney would have no problem getting him off with the hicks in Louisiana."

"Is it really that easy?" I asked.

"Of course not," Ida Belle said. "Contrary to popular belief, everyone in this state is not an idiot—except the politicians—but that doesn't stop people in other states from thinking it's so."

"So if we assume his wife knows enough to put two and two together on her husband's affair," I said, "and Ryan thinks he can walk on the murder charges, then what does he think Pansy has that he's desperate to get hold of?"

Ida Belle shook her head. "Pictures? Financial records? Something bad enough to risk coming here."

"Nothing like that was in the journal," I said. "If Pansy had something on him, it's probably back in LA."

"But he doesn't know that," Ida Belle said.

I nodded. "So you think we should tell Carter to stake out Celia's house?"

Ida Belle shook her head. "So he can tell us to stay out of his investigation? The police already let Ryan get away once. The only people heavily invested in clearing your name are the ones in this room."

"As much as I hate to agree," Gertie said, "she's right. Carter's a good boy, but he's as stubborn as a mule. Still, if we don't give him an opportunity to catch Dr. Ryan, it's not going to look good on any of us."

Ida Belle sighed. "As much as I'd like to shake that boy sometimes, I don't want to put his job in jeopardy. I'll give him a call."

She dialed and chatted for a minute—but not about Ryan—then slipped the phone back into her pocket with a smile. "Apparently, the AC at the sheriff's department has been repaired and Carter is in one of the rooms with Mark and Joanie. He gave explicit instructions to Myrtle that he was not to be disturbed."

"Whoohoo!" Gertie yelled. "Green light."

I felt a little less enthusiastic than Gertie. Granted, we'd made an attempt to contact the "proper authorities," but somehow I doubted that Ida Belle's halfhearted call to Myrtle would register as sufficient on Carter's scale.

"Get moving," Ida Belle said. "We have maybe ten minutes until Celia leaves and another twenty until it's completely dark. He'll wait until then, but we need to get in place beforehand. If he was the guy Fortune chased last night, he's already figured out that scene at the hotel was staged. If he sees us, he won't make a move."

I started to run upstairs then hesitated. "Weapons?"

Ida Belle frowned. "That's a good question as it seriously ups our trouble factor. Bring your nine, but do not use it unless he's going to kill someone."

I nodded and dashed upstairs for my pistol, then hurried back down and snagged my still-damp shoes from the back porch. Ida Belle and Gertie were nowhere in sight, so I headed outside and found them digging around in my garage.

"What are you looking for?" I asked.

Ida Belle held up a length of rope, and Gertie lifted a mass of netting.

"We figured Marge had some items we could use to improvise," Ida Belle explained as she tossed the items into the backseat of the car.

I climbed in and Ida Belle took off toward

Marie's house. "Why does Marge have a trapping net that large? Does she hunt bear?"

Ida Belle and Gertie laughed. "That net wouldn't hold bear for a second," Gertie said. "It's a cast net. You throw it out on the water, then pull it in to get bait shrimp for fishing. But with a little ingenuity, it might be enough to trip up a human."

This time, Marie prepared for our arrival by moving her own car out of her garage and allowing us to pull in. That way, if Ryan was watching the house, he wouldn't see us approach as the tinted windows on the Cadillac made it almost impossible to see inside. And more importantly, Gertie wouldn't be required to cover the distance from remote parking to Marie's house on foot.

As soon as we pulled into the garage, Marie informed us that Celia had left just minutes before. We waited until the garage door was all the way down before climbing out of the car, and then Ida Belle started barking orders at everyone.

"He won't try a break-in from the front," Ida Belle said. "Too much light. The back door is solid oak and the windows off the den have rosebushes in front of them. He'll use the window in the breakfast nook."

I nodded. So far, it made sense.

"Fortune, I want you in the back behind the blackberry bushes in case he breaks into a run. He won't risk the street, but the swamp behind the house is the perfect escape plan. I assume a six-foot wooden fence won't slow him down."

"Probably not," I said, recalling the way he'd disappeared on me.

"I'll put the net under the window and toss some

leaves on top of it. The window is at the corner of the house, closest to Marie's fence, so Gertie will sit in the tree that runs the property line and wait for him to step in the net. Then she'll pull. I'll be hiding on the other side of the steps and I'll tackle him. If he gets away, then Fortune will run him down."

I blinked. Compared to a CIA mission, this idea sounded more like a Three Stooges episode than a plan to catch a murderer, but then I supposed the fancy gadgets and equipment we used now at the agency weren't available during Vietnam when Ida Belle and Gertie got all their spy knowledge.

"What if he has a gun?" I asked, noting the big missing item in Ida Belle's calculation.

"The only way he could have gotten one is by stealing it," Ida Belle said, "and if someone's gun had come up missing, all of Sinful would have heard about it already."

It didn't sound like a firm enough argument to risk a gunshot, especially considering he'd already stolen a car or he couldn't have gotten here. But Ida Belle was acting cagey, and I got the impression there was something she wasn't telling me. Knowing I'd never get it out of her, I just nodded. Maybe she had a death wish. Maybe she planned on shooting him herself and didn't want me to know lest I then be involved in a premeditated attempted murder plot.

Bottom line: I was probably better off not knowing.

"Everyone understand their assignment?"

Marie raised her hand. "What about mine?"

"You watch from the upstairs window. As soon as we have him, you call the sheriff's department and tell Carter to get here ten minutes ago."

Ida Belle clapped her hands. "Places, people. Move, move, move."

Chapter Twenty-One

Marie dashed up the stairs as Gertie, Ida Belle, and I went out the back door. Gertie pulled and jumped at the tree several times before Ida Belle and I lifted her up onto the branch, Ida Belle shaking her head the entire time. Then Ida Belle and I scaled the fence into Celia's back yard, and I took my spot behind the blackberry bushes while Ida Belle set up the net and tossed the rope up to Gertie, who looped it around the branch above her.

The sun was sinking fast, barely a sliver left peeking over the tops of the cypress trees. The streetlights blinked on, and I knew it was only a matter of minutes before all natural light was extinguished and we'd be cast into darkness. Ida Belle had loosened the lightbulb on Celia's back door light, so only the dim glow from the kitchen filtered out onto the lawn. It was just enough for us to see Ryan, but not so much that he would see us.

I crouched down and my body instantly responded by assuming a comfortable position for a long-term stakeout. If needed, I could stay in this position for hours without cramping or aching, but if Ryan were going to show, I knew we wouldn't be waiting that long. He had to take his chance while Celia was out of the house.

The last bit of sunlight disappeared over the tree line, and the sounds of night creatures started echoing across the backyard from the swamp. I brushed an ant off my arm and scanned from Ida Belle's position to Marie's upstairs window. I couldn't see her, but I knew she was up there watching, cell phone in hand. For that, I was glad. This entire setup had the potential to go bad quickly.

Probably another ten minutes passed before I heard movement behind me. The blackberry bushes were positioned under the edge of an oak tree, so not even moonlight reached my hiding place, but I lowered myself even more in case his eyes had acclimated to the dark conditions. I peered through the blackberry bushes and watched as a faint stream of moonlight illuminated a large figure as it slid over the back row of fence and into Celia's yard.

Showtime.

My pulse ticked up a notch as he crept across the lawn. He paused about ten feet from the back of the house, and I figured he was assessing his options. Fortunately, he followed Ida Belle's train of thought and moved toward the booby-trapped window. I inched to the edge of the blackberry bush and placed both hands flat on the ground, preparing to spring like a sprinter.

My pulse spiked as he crept up to the window, and I prayed that Ida Belle and Gertie executed everything with perfect timing.

As soon as his hands touched the window, Gertie pulled.

The net wrapped around his feet like a charm, trapping him in place. Ida Belle sprang up and jumped across the steps, attempting to tackle him. Unfortunately, Gertie chose that moment to lose her balance, and fell backward out of the tree.

The rope must have hooked on to her as she dropped because all of a sudden, the intruder's feet flew out from under him and straight up into the air, yanking him upside down into the tree.

Gertie and the intruder both screamed, and he thrashed about so much I expected the net to break at any moment. I leapt up from my hiding spot and ran for the house, intent on helping Ida Belle wrestle him to the ground before he could get away. As I reached the fray, Ida Belle pulled out a curling iron and poked him in the ribs with it. He screamed bloody murder as a sizzle of electricity went off, then the thrashing stopped.

We spun him around so that we could see his face, and gave each other a satisfied smile as we gazed on the contorted face of Dr. Ryan.

"You did this with a curling iron?" I asked, starting to rethink my aversion to girlie products.

"Stun gun," Ida Belle said. "Looks like a curling iron, which makes it quite handy to carry. No one suspects you're packing."

Gertie yelled and brought us back to reality. Since it appeared that Ida Belle had the situation under control, I hopped up on the fence and saw Gertie, hanging by her feet from the other end of the rope.

"Gertie's acting as a counterweight," I said. "That's why he's still up there."

"If Gertie's the one keeping him up there," Ida

Belle said, "she needs to drop a few pounds."

"I heard that!" Gertie yelled.

A police siren sounded in the distance and a second later, Marie rushed out the back door.

"Don't just stand there," Gertie said. "Someone get me down from here."

"I think we ought to wait until Carter gets here," Ida Belle said and grinned. "No chance of Ryan getting away as long as he's dangling from the tree."

"You heard the boss," I said, trying not to smile.

"Well, he better hurry," Gertie complained. "My boobs haven't been this high up since my thirties. They're going to suffocate me."

The siren grew closer, then stopped in front of Marie's house. I heard a truck door slam and Marie directing Carter to the backyard. He ran around the corner of Marie's house and slowed just a second as he caught sight of me sitting on the fence. Then he yanked open the gate and hurried into Celia's backyard.

He took one look at the dangling Dr. Ryan and his jaw dropped.

"We tried to call you earlier," Ida Belle said, before he could start yelling. "But Myrtle said you weren't to be disturbed."

"So you thought…you know that's not…I…never mind. Help me pull him down enough to cuff him."

Ida Belle grabbed hold of his shoulders and tugged the still-groaning doctor down far enough for Carter to place him in handcuffs.

"Okay," Carter said and pulled out a knife. "I'll cut him loose."

"No!" Ida Belle, Gertie, Marie, and I all yelled at the same time.

"We have a bit of a situation here," I said and gestured to the other side of the fence.

Carter pulled himself up enough to peer over the fence and stared. His lips quivered and I could tell he was struggling not to smile.

"Fine then," he said. "Pull Gertie down and cut her loose. Ryan can drop for all I care."

Completely on board with that plan, I jumped over the fence and with Marie's help, lowered Gertie to the ground and unwrapped the rope from her ankle. As soon as I let go, I heard Ryan crash to the ground on the other side of the fence and let out a string of cursing about lawsuits and crazy people.

A couple of seconds later, Ida Belle tossed the net and rope over the fence and into Marie's backyard.

"Tell you what," Carter said as he pulled Ryan through the gate, all of us trailing across the front lawn behind him. "We'll let you explain to the judge all about the mistreatment you received from citizens while you were trying to break into a private residence just days after murdering the owner's daughter."

"I didn't murder anyone!"

"Uh-huh," he said as he pushed Ryan into his truck. "You can tell me all about it when you're behind bars."

Carter climbed into his truck and looked at all of us standing on the sidewalk, his expression serious and slightly anxious. "For the obvious reasons and a couple that aren't so visible, I'd prefer if this arrest and the details surrounding it don't get out just yet.

Can I depend on you four to keep this quiet?"

"Hell yeah," Gertie said while the rest of us nodded.

Then we all gave each other high fives.

"I'm going to pretend I didn't see that," he said and pulled away.

"I need a drink," Ida Belle said as we trailed back into Marie's house.

"I need a new bra," Gertie said. "My strap broke."

I glanced over at Gertie, who had her hand under her right boob, trying to hold it in place and failing. "Now *I* need a drink."

Ida Belle's cell phone rang and she answered it. After a brief conversation, she disconnected and frowned. "The prayer is over and Celia will be heading home any minute. We should clear out of here before she catches sight of us."

We hustled to the garage and waved to Marie as Ida Belle backed Gertie's Cadillac out of the garage and headed back to my house.

"What's up?" I asked. "You have that look like you didn't tell us everything."

"It's more a feeling than anything," Ida Belle said. "Beatrice said Celia acted strange at the prayer."

"Strange how?" I asked.

"Beatrice said she seemed fine, considering, then at the end of the prayer, Celia said she was tired of being the only one who lost when it seemed other people more deserving of loss never seemed to suffer any. She said that needed to change."

"Okay," I said. "I don't claim to be a Biblical scholar or anything, but is she saying she'd rather someone else be cursed instead of her? That doesn't sound overly Christian."

"It's not," Gertie said, "and it's also a stretch from normal thought, even for Celia."

"True," Ida Belle agreed. "Don't get me wrong. Celia can be a stone bitch, but she's not usually cruel."

"Maybe this has broken her," I said. "I mean, I know how hard it was losing my mother. I can't imagine how hard it would be to lose a child."

Ida Belle nodded. "No more downer conversation. We just hand-delivered Pansy's murderer to Carter. Come tomorrow, your good name will be restored."

"Whoot!" Gertie cheered.

"You guys should come in and celebrate. I think I have a bottle of champagne left." I looked at Gertie. "You only need one hand for a champagne glass."

"You don't have to ask me twice," Gertie said.

Ida Belle's phone rang again and she answered. I could tell by her expression that it wasn't good news.

"What's wrong?" I asked as she pulled up to the curb in front of my house.

"There's a mob downtown in front of the sheriff's department," Ida Belle said. "They're calling for your arrest or Carter's resignation. Vanessa Fontleroy gathered a bunch of people after the prayer and led the charge."

Gertie bit her lip. "It's too soon for Carter to come out with the Dr. Ryan angle. He'll want to make sure he's got his bases covered before announcing it to the public, especially given the reason why Dr. Ryan killed Pansy."

Ida Belle nodded. "We should get down there and check it out. Fortune, you better sit this one out. We'll fill you in as soon as we know something."

"No problem," I said and jumped out of the car.

"Be careful. Everyone knows we're friends."

"Get inside and lock your doors," Gertie said. "We'll call when we're on our way."

I watched for a couple of seconds as they drove off, then looked across the street and saw a curtain drop back in place at Mr. Foster's house. I gave the block a quick scan, then hurried inside, where I was certain a hot shower was calling my name.

I pushed the deadbolt on the front door in place, then headed to the kitchen to draw the deadbolt on the back door, but the second I set foot in the room, I knew someone had been there recently. My eyes locked in on the small pie tin on the breakfast table with a piece of folded paper next to it. I picked up the paper and read.

Testing a new blackberry cobbler recipe. Let me know what you think.
Ally

I put the note down and walked to the back door. It was already locked, so I drew the deadbolt into place. Ally used to deliver food to Marge when she was ill, so she probably had a key. I knew Gertie and Ida Belle did, but maybe it was time to change the locks. Not that I minded any of those three letting themselves inside, but I had to wonder if any other keys to my house were clinking around pockets in Sinful.

But that was something that could wait until tomorrow. Right now, I had delicious blackberry cobbler to test. The least I could do was get to it right away. After all, Ally was my friend, and since she'd taken the time to sneak in my house and deliver baked goodies, the least I could do was give her some feedback.

I opened the refrigerator and poured a glass of milk, already smiling as I sat down at the table and stabbed my first forkful. It was still warm and the sugar granules melted as soon as they hit my tongue, mingling with the tart sweetness of the berries. When I'd been hiding behind those blackberry bushes, I'd had no idea they yielded such heavenly results.

In hardly any time at all, my fork scratched the bottom of the pie tin, and I wished I had more. I slumped back in my seat with a satisfied sigh. What a perfect ending to an odd but productive day.

I picked up my cell phone from the table and started to dial, but then figured Ally had attended the prayer and may still be around family or other Sinful residents who sided with the mob down at the sheriff's department. A text would be better. That way, if she was able to speak, she could call.

The blackberry cobbler was incredible. Thanks!

I knew I should head up to the shower, but at the moment, the kitchen chair seemed awfully comfortable. It had been an odd day, but at least the end had been satisfying. Carter could put together his case on Ryan and hopefully, in a day or two, everyone in Sinful would know that the good plastic surgeon was the culprit and not me.

I closed my eyes for a moment, thinking I might

go straight to bed after the shower, then my phone beeped. I slid my hand across the table and turned the phone where I could see the display.

What blackberry cobbler?

A cold chill ran through me and I blinked, then struggled to sit up straight. My breathing became labored, and the kitchen counters tilted to one side, then blurred. Panicked, I fumbled with the phone but it fell from my grasp, slid across the table and dropped onto the kitchen floor.

This wasn't exhaustion. I'd been drugged.

The phone beeped again and I knew Ally was trying to text me again. I had no way of knowing what I'd ingested. If I had to wait on Ida Belle and Gertie to return, they might be too late. I forced myself to concentrate on my breathing.

You're trained for this.

The controlled breathing helped steady my limbs, although they were still incredibly weak. I figured I could slide off the chair and onto the floor for the phone. I had enough mobility and strength to manage that.

Then I heard heels clicking behind me and I knew in an instant that we'd made a horrible mistake thinking this was all over with Ryan's arrest.

Chapter Twenty-Two

The heels continued around me and I looked up into the barrel of a nine millimeter held by a smiling Vanessa Fontleroy.

I blinked a couple of times, but the view didn't change, and I struggled to make sense of what was before me. "I don't understand."

"Don't you? You seem smart enough to figure it out at this point."

Years of repeated Sinful gossip rolled through my mind—Pansy's penchant for attached men, the mayor's divorce, the ex-wife who left with most of his money and wouldn't attend her niece's funeral, Celia's admonition tonight that others hadn't suffered as she had.

Holy crap! Pansy had an affair with her uncle.

"Pansy was going to blackmail him, wasn't she?" I said.

"She was going to blackmail him *again*. How do you think she got to LA in the first place? He gave his ex the bulk of his money for her signature on a nondisclosure agreement, and the old fool thought it would all be over. I tried to tell him that he couldn't trust someone like Pansy, but he wouldn't listen."

"Evidence?"

She frowned, then her expression cleared as she understood what I was asking. "She claimed she had pictures of them together, and not the family reunion variety. But I tore her room apart and still haven't found them. I wonder now if she was lying."

"Your hands," I said, my words starting to slur. "Not big enough."

"Oh, *I* didn't kill her. I heard Herbert take the call from Pansy. I pretended to be asleep, but when he left that night, I followed him to Celia's house, expecting to catch the two of them in a compromising situation." She smiled. "Imagine my surprise and delight when I looked through the kitchen window and saw him strangling that bitch."

"Why me?"

"It's not personal. But when Herbert told me about you threatening Pansy that night at the pageant rehearsal, and since you're essentially a stranger, I knew you'd make an easy target. When he got home, he was completely panicked, but I took control, as I always do. I told him that I knew. At first, he tried to deny it, but when he realized I was actually glad he'd killed her, he relaxed."

What a lovely couple.

"Goody," I managed.

"He'd been smart enough to take her cell phone, so I told him to call your house to make it look like you were the person Pansy had called around her time of death. No one would think anything of her calling Herbert earlier in the night—not with them being related and Pansy in charge of the festival."

The drunk. It was the mayor who'd called me

that night. Not some drunk at the Swamp Bar.

"The coroner would only be able to assign a range for Pansy's death," Vanessa said. "Fifteen minutes, give or take, wouldn't dissuade a jury that you'd received a call from Pansy right before her death."

"I planned on planting the cell phone in your house and then calling a tip in to the sheriff's department," Vanessa continued, "but it took me a couple of days to rustle up a spare key. Then I had to make sure you were out of the house long enough for me to set everything up and make sure you were alone."

The mob downtown.

Ida Belle said Vanessa had led the charge. It was her way of ensuring that Ida Belle and Gertie left me alone long enough for her to take action.

Vanessa frowned. "If Carter hadn't been so stubborn—insisting on evidence before your arrest—this could have all been over days ago. You would probably have been in prison the rest of your life, but you would have been alive. If anyone is to blame for this, it's Carter, for not doing his job."

"Why kill me now?" My speech was slurred almost beyond the point of recognition.

"Oh, I'm not going to kill you—at least, not that anyone will suspect. See, I typed up a confession, going on about how guilty you feel about killing Pansy and poisoning Celia. Did I mention that the old bat has to go, too? I'm starting to suspect she knows more than we ever thought."

"So," she continued, "I'm going to put this pistol in your hand, hold it up to your head, and pull the trigger. Then I'm going to plant Pansy's cell phone in your dresser drawer. It's perfect."

I tried to clench my fist, but I couldn't even force the fingers into a ball. She was right—her plan was perfect. Never in my life had I wanted to kill someone as much as I wanted to kill Vanessa right now, and for the first time, I lacked the ability.

Surely this couldn't be it. This couldn't be the sum total of my entire life—ending at a kitchen table over some pathetic man's affair with his teenage niece. A pang of regret grabbed at me and twisted my heart as if it were in a vise. All of the things I would never have time to do flooded my mind, overwhelming me.

Concentrate!

I forced the thoughts from my mind, determined to find a way to beat the monster in front of me. I may go down, but it wasn't going to be without a fight. Vanessa reached down and lifted my hand, then let it go. Surprised, I felt my muscles contract, but I forced them to release and allowed my hand to drop full force onto the table.

Some of my strength remained. It wasn't much, but if I allowed Vanessa to do all of the lifting, I might have enough strength to pull off an escape. I'd only have a second to make it happen and only one bullet to work with, but it was the only chance I had and I was determined to take it.

"Enough chatter," Vanessa said. "I need to get this show on the road and get back to my doting husband. He owes me everything now."

She moved to my right side, lifted my hand, and wrapped it around the pistol. Then she moved it to the side of my head.

"It's been nice knowing you," she said with a

laugh and moved her finger to the trigger.

At that instant, I pressed the magazine release and kicked myself backward as I twisted the pistol around, capitalizing the best I could on my weakened state. Vanessa screamed as the magazine dropped to the floor and clutched the pistol tighter, trying to reach the trigger.

It seemed it was happening in slow motion, but for me, these situations always seemed that way. Her finger connected with the trigger and I saw her knuckle whiten. I would never get the gun turned around in time, so I put my finger over hers and ducked as I pulled the trigger.

The bullet hit the wall behind me and I tumbled over backward in the chair, crashing to the floor. Immediately, I launched forward to grab the magazine before Vanessa got to it, but I'd used most of my remaining strength already. My fingertips brushed the cold plastic of the magazine as she grabbed it from my reach and reloaded the pistol.

As she leveled the gun at me, I prayed that she was an accurate shot and this was over quickly. I'd seen enough people bleed out to know that wasn't the way I wanted to go.

The shot rang out and I waited for darkness. My body tingled, but I couldn't tell if it was from the drugs or because life was slipping away from me.

"Nice shot." Gertie's voice sounded above me.

I twisted my head up and saw a blurry Ida Belle holding a pistol.

Gertie dropped down next to me and pulled up my eyelids. "She's been drugged. Vanessa was a Valium junkie. Call for airlift. We need to get her to

New Orleans."

"Celia," I said, struggling to remain conscious as the adrenaline drained out of my body. "She poisoned…"

Then everything went blank.

I was floating.

It was a strange but wonderful feeling, having no weight or gravity. Tufts of white billowed by in a bright blue sky, bursts of sunlight streaming around me. In the distance, I saw a shimmering figure moving toward me, but I wasn't afraid.

Mother.

She looked just as I remembered her—long blond hair glistening in the rays of sunlight, turquoise eyes glowing with happiness and joy.

I broke into a smile so big that my cheeks hurt from the effort. I'd waited so long to see her again…had so much to tell her.

She stepped in front of me and lifted one hand to stroke my cheek. "My baby," she said. "I love you."

"I love you, too," I said, everything I wanted to say welling up inside of my head.

But she started to fade.

Dimmer and dimmer she became, until the last speck of light disappeared into the darkening sky. Then it was all gone and I was left in the middle of nothingness.

I bolted upright, gasping for air, hands clutching my arms.

For a moment, I gazed wildly around the room.

Was I dead?

Then I saw Gertie, Ida Belle, and Ally smiling down at me.

"She's back with us." Gertie sniffed, then brushed her eyes with her hand.

"She's a tough bird," Ida Belle said, but I could see the relief in her expression.

Ally threw her arms around me and sobbed. "Oh my God! I thought you were going to die. Even when the doctors said you'd be all right, I refused to believe them until you woke up."

I hugged her back, the reality that I wasn't dead finally sinking in.

"What happened?" I said when Ally released me.

"Vanessa drugged you and tried to kill you," Ida Belle said.

"I remember that part," I said.

Ida Belle nodded. "You put up one hell of a struggle for a woman with enough Valium in her system to put a horse to sleep."

"High tolerance," I said.

"Well, it's a darn good thing," Gertie said. "When Ally told us about your text, we knew something was wrong and went hauling it back to your house. That high tolerance of yours gave Ida Belle enough time to put one well-placed bullet between Vanessa's eyes."

I smiled, the memory of Ida Belle standing above me, smoke still coming out of her gun, slowly returning.

"Celia!" I shouted as all the details flooded back to me.

"Is alive," Gertie said. "You managed to tell us she was poisoned before you passed out. Both of you took a helicopter here to New Orleans. She's going to take a little longer than you to get back up to speed, but she's going to be fine."

I slumped back in the bed. "Thank God. So is Mayor Fontleroy in custody?"

Gertie glanced at Ida Belle and shook her head. "Word about Vanessa got to him before Carter did. He took the coward's way out."

"So they're both dead?"

"Yeah, but Carter has plenty of evidence to put Pansy's case to bed. Carter cut Dr. Ryan loose with a strong admonition that in the future, he be pickier about the women he gets involved with, but the New Orleans police want to talk to him about the vehicle he 'borrowed.'"

I shook my head. "I wonder how he's going to explain it all to his wife and staff."

"Who cares?" Ally said. "Serves him right for cheating."

"Got that right," Gertie said. "Men are such trouble."

Ida Belle gave Gertie a sideways look, then looked down at me, a faint smile on her face. "Speaking of men, Carter refused to leave until your vitals were stable."

"Oh, I'm sure he was checking on Celia, too."

"Maybe, but he didn't spend last night in Celia's room."

I looked over at Gertie, figuring Ida Belle was pulling my leg, but she smiled and nodded. "He refused to leave. Caused a bit of a stink with the nurses."

I looked down and pretended to be absorbed with adjusting the plastic bracelet on my wrist. I wasn't sure how I felt about Carter taking such a personal interest in me. On one hand, it made me feel special, but on the other, it scared me, because the person Carter thought he was looking out for wasn't that person at all.

But Ida Belle and Gertie knew exactly who I was, and they'd risked a lot to save my life and clear my name.

"Thank you," I said to Ida Belle and Gertie. "I wouldn't be sitting here if it weren't for you."

Gertie sniffed again and Ida Belle looked slightly uncomfortable.

"Seems only fair that we'd bail you out," Ida Belle said, "as we sorta got you into this mess to begin with."

"The festival." With everything else going on, I'd completely forgotten the reason for my run-in with Pansy. "What are they going to do now?"

Ida Belle shook her head. "The town's operating without a mayor at the moment, so no one knows what to do. But I'm sure I can convince them of something more suitable."

I grinned.

I would bet on it.

Chapter Twenty-Three

The hospital cut me loose after a day of observation and with a promise from me that I would take it easy. Compared to the past week, anything looked easy. The first day I was back in Sinful, a constant flow of people moved through my house, piling up casseroles and baked goods and expressing their horror and sympathy over everything that had happened.

No one came right out and said, "We're sorry we thought you were a killer," but I saw enough guilty looks to know that people felt bad for making incorrect assumptions. Walter, always the practical one, brought me a crate of root beer, Scooter tagging along behind him and clutching a pitiful arrangement of handpicked flowers. When I told Scooter how lovely the flowers were, Walter winked at me.

Ida Belle and Gertie saw that everyone cleared out at a decent hour, insisting that I needed my rest. I wasn't about to argue. I had improved miles since leaving the hospital, but I still felt nowhere near normal.

According to Walter, Carter had cleared Mark

from any involvement in Pansy's murder—not that he'd ever thought Mark was involved. Mark admitted that he'd confessed because he was afraid Joanie had been the one who'd killed Pansy. Joanie was beside herself that her husband had confessed to murder to protect her, and according to the local gossip, both appalled and somewhat pleased that he'd even considered her capable.

I'd called Harrison from the hospital and almost gave him a heart attack when I relayed what had happened. He was understandably worried, especially that Director Morrow would find out about everything and yank me out. But I assured him that with all the bad guys dead, the issue would become merely a dark mark on Sinful's past, so he calmed down and made me promise, yet again, to attempt a low profile.

By the next morning, a large part of the old me had reemerged and all the people and food and condolences started to make me feel itchy and claustrophobic. Celia returned home that morning in the care of her cousin, Dorothy, who had dumped the tray of drinks on me, but Dorothy had asked for visitors to hold off a bit so that Celia could try to get her legs back underneath her. Given her age and physical conditioning, I was certain Celia was much worse for the wear than I was.

The flow of Sinful residents tapered off at lunch and I finally managed to convince Gertie and Ida Belle to head home for a bit and give me some space. As soon as they were gone, I hopped in my Jeep and drove to Celia's house. I wanted to talk to her before the parade started at her house, assuming the cousin would let me inside.

I rapped lightly on the door, just in case Celia was asleep, and several seconds later, the door flew open and Dorothy glared out at me. When she realized who I was, the irritated expression disappeared and her eyes grew moist. She launched out the door, throwing her arms around me so hard she knocked me back a step.

"Thank you so much for saving Celia," she said, partly talking, partly sobbing. "I am so sorry I blamed you for this. Please forgive me for my anger and my pride."

"It's okay," I said and patted the woman's back. "You were just looking out for Celia. I would have done the same thing in your place."

Of course, that wasn't the least bit true because I wouldn't have accused anyone of murder when it flew completely in the face of logic, but the woman was clearly distraught and I liked my rib cage in place.

Finally, she let me go and waved me inside. "Celia is resting in her bedroom, but I know she'll want to see you."

I nodded and followed her upstairs to the master bedroom. Celia was propped up on two enormous pillows, looking pale and more fragile than I'd ever seen her look before. She looked over at me as I stepped in the doorway and gave me a small smile.

I took that as an invitation and took a seat in a chair next to the bed. Dorothy slipped quietly out of the room, leaving us alone.

"How are you feeling?" I asked.

"Like I have a hangover that would cripple a Spartan."

I smiled at the sheer accuracy of her statement.

"I have to say, though," Celia said, "that I've never been so happy to feel so awful. I hear that I have you to thank for waking up to this."

"No, I didn't do anything."

"Bull. You managed, while drifting into unconsciousness, to tell Ida Belle and Gertie that I'd been poisoned. Another hour or two delaying treatment, and I would have died."

"But you didn't," I said, feeling a little uncomfortable with her appreciation.

"Thank you," Celia said quietly. "Thank you for saving my life."

"You're welcome," I said, deciding that the simplest response was probably the best.

She wagged a finger at me. "But don't think for a second that I'm going to give you an inch on Sunday. As soon as I'm back to my regular self, I intend to beat you to Francine's, even if I have to cheat to do it."

I laughed. "I'd be disappointed with anything less."

She laughed along with me, but I could see how exhausted she was. "I'm going to let you rest," I said and rose from the chair.

She nodded and I turned to leave, then I paused and looked back at her. "I'm really sorry about Pansy." And the most surprising thing was I meant it.

Her eyes misted over and she gave me a nod.

I left her house feeling better than I had in days. In fact, I was determined to spend the afternoon lying on a lawn chair in my backyard, soaking up some sun.

I had just dozed off in said chair when I heard

footsteps behind me.

"This is what I'd like to see you do the rest of the summer," Carter said.

My pulse ticked up a notch at his voice and I didn't even bother to hide my smile. "That's because you're so used to seeing me half-naked," I said and waved a hand at my bikini.

He grinned. "Maybe."

"I think you're the only person in Sinful who didn't visit me yesterday."

"Did you miss me?"

Not about to admit that I had, I shook my head. "I didn't have time to. I greeted more people yesterday than Pastor Don does on Sunday."

"Sounds like a busy day."

"Too busy. I prefer things quiet."

"Ha! You could have fooled me."

He had a point.

"Hey," I said, "You never really thought I'd killed Pansy, did you?"

"No. I thought you were capable but I didn't think she presented a big enough challenge."

"Too bad a long string of men can't say the same thing."

He nodded. "The whole thing is surreal. Despite the fact that I think I would have figured it all out eventually, I never would have guessed in the beginning that Fontleroy and his wife were responsible and certainly not why."

"The whole thing is beyond gross, and sad for Celia."

"But maybe not without a small payoff."

"Oh?"

"I stopped by Celia's house before I came here.

Her sister was there and it looks like they're on their way to mending fences. I guess now that the truth is out, she doesn't have a reason to stay away."

I smiled, happy that Celia would get a silver lining out of all of this misery. "That's great. So I guess the sheriff is out a boss."

"For the time being. It was an election year anyway, so the city council has decided they'll take over until a new mayor is elected."

I nodded. "I might be working on the campaign for a new candidate."

His eyes widened. "Not..."

"Oh yeah," I said, delighting in his dismay. "Ida Belle figures she's been running Sinful since the sixties, so she may as well get the title and salary."

"Good God."

I couldn't have said it better myself.

The End

The Author

Jana DeLeon grew up among the bayous and gators of southwest Louisiana. She's never stumbled across a mystery like one of her heroines but is still hopeful. She lives in Dallas, Texas with a menagerie of animals and not a single ghost.

Visit Jana at:

Website: http://janadeleon.com
Facebook: http://www.facebook.com/pages/Jana-DeLeon-Author/312667975433458
Twitter: @JanaDeLeon

Books by Jana DeLeon

Rumble on the Bayou
Unlucky

The Ghost-in-Law Series:
Trouble in Mudbug
Mischief in Mudbug
Showdown in Mudbug

The Miss Fortune Series:
Louisiana Longshot
Lethal Bayou Beauty

The Indie Voice

For indie book reviews, book sales, information for indie writers, and overall good fun, visit The Indie Voice website and subscribe to our newsletter!

http://theindievoice.com/